My love of wi[illegible] time of my retirement in 2005. Since then, I have written in various genres, including children's stories, local church history, and biography on caring for my sick wife, who suffers from multiple sclerosis. Writing at this late stage in my life has been a learning curve but, overall, an enjoyable experience.

This latest fictional book is a new venture for me, and after much hesitation, I decided that writing a novel may be a positive way to include some aspects of the Christian faith. Many books and dramas on television usually give the impression that Christianity is irrelevant and rarely depict it positively.

Some good dramas and novels are spoiled by the frequent use of bad language, offensive sexual scenes, and over-the-top violence, all in the name of realism, which tends to degrade the reader and not entertain. My favourite fictional books and television dramas are mostly written before the 1960s. With these thoughts in mind, I have tried to write an interesting and exciting novel minus bad language, couples hopping into bed, and unnecessary violence. The book's main aim is to share an interesting story and, at the same time, hopefully, challenge the reader with the relevance of Christianity, which too often gets bad press.

- Les Yates -

LES YATES

THE STRANGE ABDUCTION OF JACKIE MITCHELL

This edition first published in paperback by
Michael Terence Publishing in 2023
www.mtp.agency

ISBN 9781800945937

Michael Terence
Publishing

Contents

1
Missing

The gale howled across the moor, at times whistling, whining, and making other strange and haunting sounds. David shivered, setting his teeth into an uncontrollable chatter and he wished he could find shelter from the hostile, penetrating wind. At two o'clock in the morning, it was hardly the right time or place to be exposed to the elements in such flimsy clothing.

David had found himself on the part of the Pennine moor and the middle of nowhere due to unforeseen events back home in Oxenhope. Only the day before, life had been peaceful and undisturbed. David enjoyed spending time with his seventeen-year-old daughter, who had been staying with him during the Christmas break. He had been looking forward to re-joining Jackie and spending an evening watching their favourite TV programmes. Her mum lived in Worsthorne near Burnley and had been happy to allow their only daughter to spend a few days with her dad. Though David and Sarah were separated, they stayed on friendly terms, both acknowledging that they needed to spend some time apart to help them think more about the future of their 19 years of marriage.

The mobile phone in David's inside pocket had failed to pick up a signal, making him feel even more isolated and a bit panicky. Still, he was determined to continue his search for his missing adorable daughter, Jackie. The note she had left behind informed him that Mum was feeling desperately unwell and had asked her to come quickly. Jackie's only alternative to reach the isolated old farmstead was a five-mile walk across the moor. Having phoned for the local doctor to attend to her mum, she felt no hesitation in making her way by the quickest route across the moor she knew so well. The frightening thing for David was that his wife had already phoned him to say the doctor had arrived, but there was no sign of Jackie.

The boggy ground was now hindering David from making much progress. The occasional break in the night clouds allowed a full moon to expose the empty wilderness revealing no signs of Jackie. David continued to call out for his beloved daughter, but his loud shouts received no response, making David more and more anxious and deeply worried for her safety. He eventually made it across the unforgiving terrain with no success in finding Jackie. When he stumbled into the courtyard of his wife's humble dwelling, he was shaking with fear and clung to Sarah. Despite his being cold and wet, she held him tightly to her. Allowing David to get warm before the log fire, Sarah delayed telling him that there had been no response from Jackie's mobile phone despite her trying to call their daughter most of the night.

David and Sarah spent the remaining hours of the night sitting together on the settee in utter despair, having decided to resume their search at the first sign of light. This would not arrive until late, being the 23rd of December. David suggested that Sarah remain at the farmstead to be on hand should Jackie return, although both thought the chance of that was remote. Sarah had already informed the local police station of their missing daughter, but apart from a promise to 'look into it' by the desk sergeant, frustratingly, there had been no further response.

2

Desperation and despair

The snow began falling as David set off again across the moor. The extra coat belonging to his wife failed to zip up due to it being a couple of sizes too small but did help a little. He was undeterred by the cold and damp conditions and determined to search the moor for as long as it took. It took most of the day, and it was already dark by four o'clock in the afternoon. David was now not far from his home and decided to have something to eat, put on warmer clothing, and resume his search.

Hoping against hope that Jackie had already returned home, David stumbled into the welcoming warmth of his home and proceeded to look in every room in the house. There was no Jackie. He slumped into his chair, totally exhausted. The tears began to flow as little hope of finding Jackie dawned on his anguished soul.

The ringing of his mobile phone brought his sobbing to a halt. As he fumbled with trembling fingers to answer the call, the phone slipped from his hands, and before he could retrieve it, the ringing stopped. Frantically tracing the caller's number, he found to his utter joy that the call had come from Jackie's mobile. Still trembling, David returned her call only to find the calling tone continued to ring with no answer. Having informed Sarah of what had transpired, David tumbled into his bed, fully-clothed and worn out, and fell into a fitful sleep.

He awoke abruptly to the familiar tune on his mobile phone. Again, it was from Jackie but, much to his consternation, the caller remained silent apart from the sound of heavy breathing.

"Who are you, and where is my daughter?" hollered David as the heavy breathing continued.

Then it occurred to him that the heavy breathing might be Jackie and, in desperation, exclaimed,

"Is that you, Jackie? Are you in trouble?"

"Dad…"

The faltering weak reply was from Jackie, and to David's absolute horror, the phone went dead. The battery on his phone had run out of power. Fumbling for the battery charger with shaking hands, he managed to connect the phone on recharge, bringing it back to life. However, calling her number brought no response and as the phone's ringing tone remained unanswered, David collapsed on the floor in a despairing heap. When the phone rang again, he jumped to his feet and, quickly pressing it in answer mode to his ear, found that it was Sarah. Between sobs, he told her what had just transpired, and she suggested they try to trace the phone's location.

"Of course!" howled David. "How foolish of me not to think of that."

He blew Sarah a kiss and proceeded to use the

tracing app to locate exactly where the phone was. The result of his search caused even more anguish and consternation; the app was telling David that the phone was not very far from Carlisle!

3

A mad dash north

Even though it was now approaching midnight, David wasted no time in reaching the drive and jumping into his car. He set the satnav for Warwick Bridge on the A69 just outside Carlisle and having checked his phone to see that the tracker continued to indicate this location, he headed north towards the M6. It took David all his composure to remain within the speed limit, but he was soon touching 80 the moment he joined the M6 thinking the chance of being caught breaking the speed limit was worth the risk. The flashing lights of the police car ahead brought a wail from David. The traffic behind the police car had to slow down due to a hold-up. The hold-up was caused by an accident involving a three-car pile-up meaning that the motorway traffic was going nowhere.

Fortunately, he was not far from the slip road leading to Penrith and, to the irritation of the other motorists, meandered his way down the slip road. After driving through the centre of Penrith, he joined the A6 north. Fifteen miles later, he was approaching his destination. The tracker led David down an unlit country lane, very bumpy and dark. He managed to avoid a lone deer as it darted across the lane in full view of the car's headlights giving him quite a start. David had now reached the phone's location, a deserted, ruined farmhouse. His heart pounded as he jumped from the car.

The doorway, minus a door, led into a large empty room. David shone his mobile torch slowly, revealing nothing, only an old wooden staircase that led to an upper floor. He had to tread carefully on the way up, as several steps were missing. At the top, he peered into the upper room and discovered a large wooden linen box. David's heart was now almost jumping out of his chest as he hesitated to open it. Slowly lifting the creaking lid and shining in his torch revealed nothing. Much to his relief, it was empty, but where was the phone? All was quiet until he decided to ring Jackie's number, and the familiar ringing tone began to play. The phone's sound came from above, and as David shone his torch upwards, he saw an opening in the loft.

He scrambled to get the linen box underneath the loft's open space and, with outstretched arms, managed to grip the frame and hoist himself high enough to prize himself into the pitch darkness of the loft. The phone was ringing loud and clear, with its light shining in the darkness. David could see that the loft was completely empty. Retrieving the phone, he fell awkwardly onto the linen box ending up on the floor, which caused a hefty jolt to his lower back. He lay there, taking time to get his breath back, thinking himself fortunate to still be in one piece and able to make his way slowly back to the car. Having rested, David continued to search the area around the farmhouse and was now convinced that wherever Jackie might be, she was not in the isolated farmhouse in the middle of nowhere.

4

A tragic car chase

Having contacted Sarah to inform her of his futile search, David was making his way along the bumpy dirt track when headlights appeared in the distant darkness. The oncoming saloon car made an abrupt stop, swerved left, reversed, and sped off at breakneck speed back up the track towards the A6. David followed in hot pursuit. The Fiesta must have been doing at least seventy miles per hour as it made its way through the deserted streets of Penrith before joining the M6 motorway. David followed, and both cars soon touched a hundred miles an hour. David was in no fit state to be driving at this speed, having been deprived of sleep for the last 48 hours but was determined to keep the Fiesta in sight. The madness continued as far as the Kendal slip road, where the car suddenly swerved in a last-minute attempt to lose its pursuer. David had plenty of time to follow but, to his horror, he then watched as the Fiesta took off, leaving the road and taking flight over an embankment and hitting a large tree head-on.

David brought his car to a shuddering halt and jumped out, trembling from head to foot; his great fear now was to find Jackie in the smouldering crumpled wreck. There was no Jackie, but a young man was in the driving seat, still alive but only just. David did not have to call the emergency services as a passing motorist had already done so. In the meantime, David was trying desperately to keep the injured driver calm, assuring him that the ambulance was on its way. The young lad beckoned David to put his head near his mouth and, on doing so, whispered in his ear that he had been sent by a man from Burnley to retrieve the phone; he had offered him three hundred pounds. David just about heard what the young lad was saying, but before he could gain any more information, the lad slumped forward and, as far as David could see, was now dead. Before the paramedics arrived to confirm that the young lad had died from his injuries, David searched the lad's pockets to find what he was hoping to find, a mobile phone.

David made his way down the M6, having left his details with the police attending the crash site; he would be needed as a witness to the incident later. He decided to make his way to Sarah's and, after greeting her and telling her all that had happened, he fell into a deep sleep on her sofa. It was seven in the morning when he awoke. Opening his bleary eyes, he saw Sarah sitting beside him on the sofa; she had been busy making scrambled eggs on toast and a mug of hot coffee, which David gratefully received. They were already discussing what had transpired during the night and, with great anticipation, began to examine the contents of the young man's phone. The last call had been made to Jackie's phone, but it was the previous one that David was most interested in. Could this lead to the whereabouts of Jackie? He was devastated to find that the call had come from a public phone box.

However, in the list of contacts on the lad's phone, David and Sarah could trace and verify each contact consisting of friends and family, but there was one name, Afrim Belushi, which could not be accounted for. Doing some research on the internet, David learned that the name was of Albanian extraction. It was little to go on, but it was all they had, and after some lunch, they made their way to Burnley police station on Parker Road in the centre of town.

5
Afrim Belushi

The desk sergeant was much more cooperative this time, having heard the length of time Jackie had been missing. After consulting Chief Inspector Braddock, they set up their investigation to trace Jackie's whereabouts. David and Sarah felt much more relieved now that the police were involved in trying to find their beloved daughter.

The procedure was much more intense than David had anticipated; the first part involved searches of his and Sarah's homes. They informed him they would also be searching the area, checking hospitals, Jackie's mobile phone and computer, and all CCTVs in the area. They realised that David would want to have Jackie's mobile on hand and, after taking details, returned it to him, much to his and Sarah's relief. In the meantime, David did not mention the contact number belonging to Afrim Belushi, deciding to make his own investigation, and neither did he mention where Jackie's mobile was retrieved from. Sarah had doubts about not revealing this information to the police but went along with David's hunch that this was the best plan.

Sarah wasn't feeling well and decided to return to her home in Worsthorne, leaving David to try to trace Afrim Belushi's whereabouts. Having made inquiries at the Town Hall, David learned that there was a community of migrants scattered in various B&Bs in the town, involving a few Albanians. Plodding the streets of Burnley and trying to locate these migrants took time and patience, but his patience paid off when he found a couple of Albanians who knew of Afrim Belushi. They were rather reticent in opening up and sharing information on Belushi. Still, after the offer of fifty pounds each, they informed David that he was involved in a drug gang that had recently moved into the area. The two Albanians even had an address, and after David assured them that he would be silent on the source of his information, he thanked them and made his way to the other side of the town to find this elusive mystery man.

David soon arrived at his destination, and standing outside the flats with his heart beating fast, he entered the main entrance and proceeded up the stairs to look for flat number 23. He had already phoned Sarah to update her on his progress and told her that if he did not phone her again within thirty minutes, she should inform the police of his location immediately.

He waited outside the flat for a moment, then, with trepidation, knocked on the door. It moved slightly and David found it was unlocked. As he slowly opened it, he was met with a strong, pungent odour. The room was in darkness, and fumbling to find a switch, David stumbled headlong over an object on the floor, banging his head on a solid table leg. Feeling quite dazed, he gasped in horror after regaining his senses; the object on the floor was a motionless body. David managed to get himself in a standing position and, with the light coming in from the open door, began to examine the body for any signs of life; the absence of pulse indicated that the man he had fallen over was dead. The man's pockets revealed a wallet, a passport, and a wad of twenty-pound notes. The name on the passport was Afrim Belushi.

Much to his horror, amongst these items, David also found Jackie's credit card, which caused him to shake with panic. He staggered to his feet, shakily descended the stairs, and left the building. Finding a Starbucks close by, David went in and tried to regain his composure. As he sat there drinking a welcome Nitro cold brew coffee, hoping the caffeine would help to gather his thoughts, he remembered his need to phone Sarah. Fortunately, there were very few customers close at hand as David related to Sarah all that had happened in flat 23, omitting to mention the credit card so as not to cause Sarah much more worry.

6

Detective Constable Matthew Peterson

The town of Burnley was bustling with Christmas Eve shoppers as David drove back to Worsthorne to join Sarah. The snow was still falling, making the hills white, and in normal circumstances, a white Christmas would have made the ideal festive setting for David, Sarah, and Jackie, but those plans were now in tatters. The hug from Sarah that greeted David was so warm and lovely, making them both wonder why they had ever agreed to spend the last two months apart. The warm cheeks of Sarah pressing on the cold cheeks of David took a long time to separate as they clung tightly, not wanting to let each other go.

Eventually, they sat down, and Sarah updated David on the latest news from the police, which had revealed very little, and the term used by the desk sergeant was 'ongoing.'

Sitting on the sofa, David began to examine the contents of the wallet retrieved from the corpse. Tucked away in one of the compartments, he found a folded piece of paper with markings drawn in pencil. There were squiggly lines and arrows all pointing to a cross marked in the centre of the sheet. David's mind began to race, wondering whether this roughly-drawn map indicated where Jackie was hidden. Sarah tried her best to be more positive, saying that the map could be anything, but even she felt the knot inside her stomach as she realised how significant it could be. As tears streamed down the cheeks of David, Sarah, too, began to sob. The only course now, they both agreed, was to share everything they knew with Chief Inspector Braddock. David contacted the Police Station in Burnley, requesting that they call in at Sarah's as soon as possible, adding that they had important information on the case.

David arose from the sofa the following day and remembered it was Christmas. Sarah was already up and busy in the kitchen preparing breakfast. After a quick wash and shave, he hurried from the bathroom and joined Sarah in the dining room, where breakfast of hot porridge and toast was waiting. They sat in silence as they ate. He glanced across at her between sips of coffee and watched a tear drop onto her blouse. There was only one tear as Sarah was determined to keep composed and in control. He reached across the table, holding tightly to her hand and with as much love and compassion as he could muster, wished her a very happy Christmas and tried to assure her that whatever it took, they would find Jackie.

Much to their surprise, a young policeman in plain clothes called in at Sarah's home the same day; they did not expect anyone to come until after the Christmas break. The policeman was Detective Constable Peterson, who reminded David of Sergeant Lewis of the popular television detective drama, Morse. Funnily enough, he spoke with a Geordie accent when he introduced himself. Peterson had a kind, assuring approach. After expressing much sympathy over the awful ordeal of their daughter's disappearance, he put on latex gloves and examined the wallet and its contents. Peterson had already informed headquarters to make no delay in locating the body of Afrim Belushi, he would visit the crime scene later, but just now, he was more interested in tracing the last time and place where the credit card had been used and any fingerprints or DNA on each item.

Peterson's other chief concern was whether Belushi had kidnapped Jackie and hidden her away somewhere and had somehow met his death, taking the secret of her whereabouts with him. However, Peterson kept these thoughts to himself. Everything was conjecture just now, and having promised David and Sarah that he would do all within his power to find Jackie, he returned to police headquarters.

The following day, Boxing Day, Peterson rang, asking David and Sarah if they would like to join him at the police station. One of the main reasons was for David to be fingerprinted to sort out the prints on the items belonging to Belushi. But also, Peterson knew that they would be agitated and unsettled and hoped to involve them in some crime detection. Peterson realised that it was unconventional, but as there was limited staff in the station and Chief Inspector Braddock wasn't around as he was on holiday, he felt it was the least he could do to keep David, and Sarah's minds occupied. When they did arrive, Peterson shook their hands and made room for them in his cramped office. He also informed them that the initial report on Belushi's death was a drug overdose, which seemed unintentional.

David and Sarah learned a lot about Peterson during their visit. He had moved down from Newcastle; he was twenty-three years of age and had only been in the job of Detective Constable in Burnley for three months; before that, he served as a policeman in Sunderland and had been highly thought of, the Sunderland force was sorry to see him go. They also learned that he lived in rented digs near Townley Park. He was also happy to be working over the Christmas break to avoid the loneliness of living in an unfamiliar town with few friends.

Peterson needed to get to know more about Jackie, especially her friends and social habits. Her Facebook page and contacts on Messenger and Instagram would all need to be checked. He planned to visit the high school where Jackie was a pupil, but that would have to wait until the school reopened after the holiday. As they chatted, David and Sarah warmed to Peterson, who insisted they use his first name, Matthew, in fact, just Matt would be fine. He informed them that a thorough search of the moor, both by police on the ground and by helicopter, had been unable to trace any sign of Jackie and that house-to-house inquiries were still happening in the local area. He asked if he could have another look at Jackie's bedroom, and together, they drove back to Sarah's house, where Sarah insisted that they all had some refreshments, which she had prepared earlier, of which there was plenty enough for Matt to share.

7

Hopes dashed

Whilst Sarah was washing up, her mobile phone rang. Quickly wiping her hands on the tea towel, she picked up the phone and swiped the answer mode in time to hear Jackie's anxious cry,

"Mum!"

There was nothing else, only the click of a receiver at the other end, terminating the call. Matt and David had already leapt from their chairs. Matt grabbed the phone first and finding the caller's number, re-dialled. It rang and continued to ring. After what seemed like an eternity, two or three minutes, a woman's voice answered,

"Hello?"

"Who is this?" asked Peterson.

"I think you may have the wrong number," she replied. "This is a public call box in Piccadilly Station, Manchester. I was just passing, so out of curiosity decided to answer it."

"This is the police. Did you see anyone else use the phone?" asked Peterson.

"There was a young couple close by, but they've just boarded a train. I think it's going to Glasgow."

"Can you describe the young lady and what she was wearing?" he asked again, anxiously.

"She had dark hair and was wearing what looked like a Parka, a light green long coat, the man had fair hair, and I think he may have been wearing blue jeans and a short blue jacket; those are the only details I can remember."

Peterson thanked her and asked for her contact details, but she ended the phone call without an answer.

David and Sarah confirmed to Peterson that Jackie was wearing a Parka as described. After checking the source of the phone call, that it was indeed a public call box situated in Piccadilly Station, they were full of mixed emotions. If the young lady was Jackie, then at least she was alive.

Though Peterson didn't like to disturb Chief Inspector Braddock's holiday, he needed to ask his permission to arrange contact with British Transport police based at Piccadilly Station. His request was to quickly seal the telephone kiosk off from further use by the public and inform the transport police on duty at the various stations on the Manchester-Glasgow line. Given the descriptions of the missing couple, he hoped that Jackie would now be found, as well as the person accompanying her. Having given Peterson's urgent request some heart-searching thought, Braddock contacted Chief Constable Watson of Lancashire Constabulary for advice, who immediately complied with all the necessary arrangements.

"Come on, let's get down to Piccadilly Station. We can't sit here twiddling our thumbs," declared Matt, jumping up from his seat.

David and Sarah were all too willing and in no time found themselves speeding up the M65 in a police car with blue light flashing and heading for Manchester. The police patrol car made good time despite the icy conditions, and by the time the trio had entered Piccadilly Station, there were no transport police to be seen. A policeman stood guard, preventing any access to the particular public telephone booth. David and Sarah were impressed by young Peterson looking official and conversing with one policeman who seemed to be coordinating the operation. David and Sarah then saw Peterson shaking his head and looking slightly embarrassed. He walked over to David and Sarah with drooping shoulders and, with a deep sigh, said,

"No trains are running today due to an all-out strike by the RMT Rail Union. It seems like the mystery lady who used that public telephone is playing some game with us and may be responsible for your daughter's disappearance."

8

An account of what really happened to Jackie

The date was the 23rd of December, and Jackie's phone rang, indicating that her mum was calling.

"Jackie, I don't feel well. It would be helpful if you could stay the night with me. If you get a taxi, I will pay the fare."

Jackie made no hesitation in ringing around for a taxi but received the same response each time she rang,

"Sorry, fully booked for the next few hours."

Jackie zipped up her Parka, left a note for Dad, and made her way to the moor. The time was four o'clock in the afternoon, and it was already getting dark, but Jackie was well prepared, having her mobile phone tucked in her pocket. As she was crossing the road that led to open ground and the moor, an oncoming car flashed its headlights.

"Oh good," she thought, "looks like dad."

The car, which was the same model as her dad's, pulled up, and before Jackie realised what was going on, she was manhandled into the back seat by two men and driven away at breakneck speed. She was terrified. The hood placed over her head smelt musty, but at least she could breathe through the mesh fabric. She heard a lady, who appeared to be driving the car, instruct the older, larger man to tie Jackie's hands, to which he replied in broken English that he had nothing to tie her with.

"Idiot!" replied the woman, in perfect English. "Use your tie."

"Me have no tie, lady."

"Use your belt then and your brains."

"Pants come down if do that."

"Use your belt, and don't argue!"

Jackie's hands hurt, but the pain was relieved when the burly man retied the belt slightly looser.

The car seemed to drive on forever. Jackie's heart had been beating hard the whole of the journey, and the two or three captors hardly exchanged a word all the way. Finally, after a bumpy last couple of miles, the car came to a stop. Jackie was bundled out of the car without much consideration for her delicate frame and, once inside the building, was carried up some steps into an upper room and then all was silent.

Jackie was relieved that they had not bothered to search her and felt the shape of her mobile phone still in her inside Parka pocket. It was a relief to be relieved of the belt around her wrists and the smelly hood that had been wrapped around her head. The room was in total darkness, but using the torch on her mobile phone,

Jackie examined her surroundings.

There was much activity early in the night downstairs, with many voices in broken English. The lady, who seemed to be monopolising the conversation, mentioned the word 'smack' quite a few times; Jackie then realised that they were discussing heroin as she had heard it being described as 'smack' in school.

The night was long. Jackie did not sleep at all and was relieved when the daylight shone through the wooden slats giving some light. A young lad with a handkerchief covering half his face popped his head around the corner and shoved a plate along the floor consisting of a piece of bread and a glass of water. Jackie assumed he must have been the lad in the car's front seat. The day dragged on with the sound of cars coming and going and much activity below.

When all was quiet again, Jackie reached for her phone and keyed in her dad's number. Much to her frustration, it remained unanswered, so ending the call quickly, she returned the phone to her inside pocket. As the darkness drew in and downstairs became silent, Jackie tried once more to ring her dad and to her sheer joy, the phone was answered. Jackie was afraid to raise her voice, but eventually and as quietly as possible, she called out,

"Dad."

The footsteps on the stairs from below caused her to immediately end the call and conceal her phone in the hidden pocket. A torch shone around the room, and when it shone on Jackie, she was already pretending to be asleep. The man retreated down the stairs, and after muttering the word mobile phone a lady's voice was raised and bellowed,

"You stupid idiot."

Jackie realised what was going to happen next and, with the help of her mobile torch, seeing the opening to the loft, threw the mobile phone up in the air, hoping it would land securely out of reach of her kidnappers. When the mobile stayed put, she sat down on the dusty floor. The foul, sweaty man could now be heard bounding up the steps, but with his pants almost round his ankles, he had to make several attempts to climb the stairs.

"You have phone?" he bawled.

"No!" replied Jackie.

The man then began to search her with one hand, holding his pants up with the other.

"Take coat off."

Jackie complied.

The man searched the Parka and then proceeded to search Jackie roughly, shining a torch in her face the whole time so she couldn't see the face of her despicable assailant.

The clatter of feet coming up the steps made Jackie jump, followed by the rough handling of our fat friend. The hood and belt were soon back in their uncomfortable place. Now, wondered Jackie, where do we go next. At least the car was warmer as it continued on its way to who knows where. As the vehicle pulled up, ending their long journey, Jackie was getting a bit fed up with being tossed to and fro like a sack of potatoes, and blurted out,

"Pity you didn't find my mobile phone, which, by the way, is in the loft in the building we have left behind."

"Idiot!" screamed the woman. "You incompetent idiot. You will have to go back for it now."

The young lad volunteered to go for some extra cash, paid for by our 'idiot' friend and the use of his clapped-out Ford Fiesta and was soon racing back up the motorway.

Unknown to Jackie, her captors had returned her to Burnley. But before they left the car, her fat friend stuck a needle in her arm, which immediately sent her into a deep sleep. Covering Jackie with a car rug, the couple went into a building, ascended the stairs and entered the flat on the third floor; the lady counted the proceeds of their ill-gotten gains obtained from the drug runners in Carlisle and handed a thousand pounds to the fat man plus a supply of heroin. He could not wait to get his fix as he had been shaking most of the journey. His lady accomplice returned to the car, unaware that the smack administered through a vein in his arm had been enough to put her accomplice into an endless sleep from which he would never wake up. The journey to Carlisle was very profitable for our mystery lady, who, after leaving the apartment block, sped off in her Audi Quatro with a sleeping Jackie in the back seat.

9

Good and bad news

Boxing Day was a normal day for Detective Constable Peterson, now back at his desk at the Burnley HQ. David and Sarah decided to stay together at Sarah's home in Worsthorne while maintaining contact with Peterson. The journey back from Manchester had been a wrench. There was nothing further they were able to do at Piccadilly Station, and could only hope that the appeal for witnesses made by Greater Manchester Police on the identity of the mystery woman would bear some fruit. There was one positive outcome, however, in that the trauma of the last few days had brought David and Sarah closer together, which helped to bear some of the anguish and worry of the abduction of their much-loved daughter, Jackie.

The following day, Peterson turned up on the doorstep of Sarah's home. He was welcomed by David and Sarah, hoping he had some good news. The news was good and bad. A witness had been found who claimed she saw a lady use the telephone around the same time as the call was made to Peterson the previous day. She remembered the lady due to her expensive outfit and the unusual feathered hat and black gloves. Another witness had also been contacted who saw the same lady remonstrating with a traffic warden over her Audi Quattro being parked in a no-parking area outside

Piccadilly Station. The same traffic warden who had recorded the incident, along with the car's registration number, had already been contacted. Further inquiries revealed that the car was seen on the M5 near Worcester later that day. Peterson had wasted no time in contacting West Mercia Police to ask for help in tracing the car. In the meantime, unfortunately, the registration number had been traced to a car written off a couple of years ago due to a road accident. This mystery woman became more elusive with each passing day.

David's heart sank as he listened to what Peterson had to say. Sarah held her head in her hands and finished up sobbing into the tea towel she had been using to wipe the breakfast crockery. Matt put a comforting arm around Sarah's shoulders and again promised them both that he would trace this woman if it took the whole UK police force to find her; a promise he knew was not very feasible.

As expected, on hearing the mystery lady had been wearing gloves, Peterson was to learn later that there were no fingerprints on or around the telephone kiosk.

10

Greenway Mansion

Jackie's head throbbed as she tried to shield the daylight from the car window. She had no idea where she was, nor was she even aware that it was Christmas Day.

"Out you get," commanded the mystery lady, and holding onto Jackie's arm, led her up some steps into a large house that could be described as more of a mansion.

Once inside, Jackie was amazed at the flamboyance and extravagance of the décor and furniture. The marble stairs and gold-painted bannister led to an upstairs landing leading to many rooms. Jackie was asked surprisingly politely by the mystery woman to enter one of these large rooms. The sitting/bedroom was filled with every conceivable item of furniture, including a large white cashmere-covered sofa, a four-poster bed, and luxury velvet curtains. The mystery lady smiled, told Jackie to make herself comfortable, and left the room, locking the door behind her.

Jackie lay on the bed, resigned to her present fate. The last few days were catching up on her. The bed felt so snug and comfortable, and she was soon in a deep and needed sleep.

A knock at the door brought Jackie back to her nightmare and she momentarily wondered where she was. The key in the lock turned, and in walked a man dressed as what can only be described as a very posh waiter. He was carrying a tray of food and drink which smelt and looked delicious.

"Her Ladyship would like you to eat now," said the visitor. "I am her Ladyship's butler and will look after you while her Ladyship is away for a few days. If there is anything you need, just pull the cord next to the display cabinet. Towels and all your toilet and washing needs are stored in the ensuite bathroom, and clean clothes are stored in the side room in the fitted wardrobes. Enjoy your dinner." And with a parting bow, the butler left the room.

The large mantelpiece clock struck seven in the evening. Jackie looked out of the expansive bay window into the darkness and saw a long drive with intermittent lamplights stretching a good mile. The food on the tray was now beckoning, and Jackie sat down and devoured the meal hungrily. She was already planning her escape as she ate the last piece of toast. Feeling much better and more alert, she began to examine the room, concentrating on the bay window. Disappointingly, the window was locked securely, but more worrying was the small camera high in the far corner of the room pointing directly at the window and totally unreachable.

The wide-screened television on the far wall would help pass the time, but for now, Jackie needed to know exactly what was happening. Pulling on the cord for the butler's attention, she did not have long to wait before the butler entered the room.

"You called, madam?"

"Yes, butler, or whatever your name is. Where am I, and why am I here?" she asked, not really expecting a logical answer.

"You are in Greenway Mansion somewhere in the middle of Somerset. The property belongs to Lady Greenway; further details I am not allowed to give, and by the way, you can call me James," replied the butler.

"You still haven't told me why I am here?" said Jackie, expecting a reply.

"That, madam, will be revealed in due course by her Ladyship when she returns. In the meantime, I suggest you make yourself comfortable." James, the butler, then left the room and locked the door.

Jackie switched on the television and tuned into the news channel. She soon got bored and was just rummaging in some drawers when her ears pricked up at the mention of Burnley. The news bulletin was now being addressed by a detective making some form of appeal. Jackie could hardly believe her ears when her name was mentioned. Chief Inspector Braddock from Burnley CID was appealing for information regarding Jackie Mitchell, a young seventeen-year-old girl last seen wearing a light green Parka jacket. He went on to say that Jackie had been missing for five days, and they were extremely concerned for her safety. Jackie was now pulling on her hair and screaming,

"I'm here!" she then fell to her knees and began to sob uncontrollably.

The following morning, the sleep, shower, and change of clothes helped Jackie feel much better. Later that morning, seeing the Audi Quattro swoop up the long drive, Sarah was full of anticipation, expecting some answers from her Ladyship, who, in Sarah's mind, was no lady.

11

Oliver Mitchell

Oliver Mitchell was enjoying his time with Barry. It was good to get away from Lancashire, thought Oliver. His relationship with his father had not been going too well lately due to his disagreement with his dad's separation from his mum. The Christmas break spent in his university digs in Durham meant that Oliver had more time with his friends and was looking forward most of all to the New Year party in the centre of Durham.

Today, Boxing Day, Oliver and Barry went to their usual haunt for a chat and an evening meal, joining more friends from the University campus. They loved to discuss the world's problems, and lively political debate was always at the forefront of any discussion. During the evening meal, two British-born students of Nigerian heritage sat across the table. Oliver had not really met these two before, and over the chatter of the thirty or so students, heard them talking to each other, planning about meeting up for church on Sunday and discussing a book on theology. Oliver gave Barry a smirk, muttering under his breath to Barry something about religion being contagious. One of the Nigerian students smiled and held out his hand to Oliver and Barry with an offer to shake their hands and introduce himself. Oliver didn't take much notice of his unpronounceable name but reluctantly held out his hand and, with a contemptuous dig, asked if they needed the prop of religion to survive student life in Durham.

"We certainly do," replied Adebamgbe, smiling. "I know this might sound silly, but do you know what it means to be a Christian?"

Oliver was quick to answer,

"It means that he or she thinks they are better than anyone else and goes to church on Sunday to get in God's good books."

"That is one way of looking at it, I suppose, but would you mind if I told you what I think it means?"

"If you must," replied Oliver, eating another mouthful of his pizza.

"Well, the first thing I would like to say is that my answer is not something that has come from my own limited resources but from the divine revelation of the Bible. Would like me to read a portion of a book I borrowed from the church library?

"What is it, Aesop's Fables?"

Oliver felt quite smug with his answer and burst out laughing. The two Nigerians could not help laughing too, showing no sign of being offended.

"What does Aesop say in your precious book?" continued Oliver.

Adebamgbe found the chapter and, over the noise of all the chatter, read from one of the paragraphs where he had placed a bookmark earlier.

"The author says that there is a marvellous unity in the Bible. It is one book, and yet it is made of sixty-six books composed by not less than forty writers. The time it took to complete the whole Bible was about sixteen hundred years. The contributors ranged from kings and scholars to herdsmen and fishermen. Despite the writers' different times and varied backgrounds, there is a wonderful symmetry and united theme throughout its pages. Holiness seems to be written on every page; its power and influence have never been surpassed by any other literature of any age.

"Theologians use the terms 'plenary inspiration' and 'verbal inspiration.' Plenary means that the Holy Spirit was the author of all the Scriptures. By verbal inspiration, they mean that the very words and thoughts of the sacred writers were guided in such a way that the writers said and wrote exactly and infallibly what God wanted them to say. The main languages God used to reveal his holy will were mainly Hebrew in the Old Testament and Greek in the New Testament. The original Manuscripts were without error and divinely inspired. However, manuscripts would have worn out over time, but for centuries faithful scribes made sure that reliable copies of the original manuscripts were produced and kept safe under the protection and providence of God Himself.

"All the participants involved in writing and speaking the original words of God acknowledge that the rest of the books that make up the Bible are divinely inspired. Jesus often referred to the Old Testament in his teachings, quoting them as authoritative. On one occasion, Jesus affirmed 'that the Scriptures cannot be broken' John 10:35, which means that they are indestructible, unalterable, and permanent."

"There are many contradictions in the Bible; how can you say there is cohesion?" interrupted Oliver, who was now forcing a smile while getting slightly agitated.

"If you are not too offended, Oliver, can I continue to explain what I think a Christian is?" Adebamgbe was now trying his best to keep the conversation light and friendly.

"If you must, but I don't want to talk about religion all evening; I am here to enjoy myself."

"Oliver, you just say the word, and I will change the topic," replied Adebamgbe.

"If you must bore us all to tears, carry on," Oliver was a bit more composed and did feel uncomfortable about his behaviour.

"A Christian," continued Adebamgbe, "according to the Bible, is one who believes in Jesus Christ that he is the promised Messiah, foretold would come in the Old Testament. All Old Testament prophesies, and animal sacrifices pointed to One who would become the ultimate sacrifice. His death on the cross was no accident but planned by God the Father so that Jesus would be an atoning sacrifice for sin. In other words, God's Son died for our sins so that we could be forgiven. Atonement really means 'at-one-ment' bringing reconciliation between a holy God and sinful human beings. Therefore, Christians believe in the inspired Word of God, believe Jesus to be their Saviour and Lord, and with God's help seek to follow what the Bible teaches."

"That's okay if you want to believe that, but it is irrelevant to me," replied Oliver. "I don't need saving, and I pride myself in being as good as the next man."

Just as Adebangbe was nervously trying to continue the conversation, the waiter approached the table and asked if they required any drinks. After a long pause and drinks ordered, Adebangbe sat silent.

"Please go on," prompted Barry.

"If that is okay with your friend, I will willingly continue the discussion. You were saying that you were as good as the next man."

Oliver nodded.

Adebangbe then smiled and said, "You probably are. But! Are you as good as God? That is the standard God requires. The Bible tells us that we have all sinned and come short of God's standard. Consequently, we all need saving from our wrongdoings, which include your thoughts and actions."

Oliver slammed his glass on the table and declared, "I have heard enough of this drivel, let's change the subject."

However, Barry, who had said nothing during the discussion, seemed moved by what he had just heard.

Later that evening, Oliver returned to his flat feeling lightheaded after having drunk more than usual. Lying on the bed, fully clothed, was just about to nod off when his phone rang.

"Oliver, it's Dad."

Oliver sat up, "Yes, Dad, what is it?"

David gave a nervous cough, "I'm afraid I have some bad news. Your sister Jackie has been abducted."

"What do you mean abducted?" gasped Oliver, trying to keep his shaking hand still.

"She was taken away in a car, and we have no idea where she is. I'm sorry I didn't tell you sooner, but I didn't want to worry you over Christmas."

Oliver screamed down the phone, "You should have told me sooner!"

The following morning, the day after Boxing Day, Oliver boarded the train for Manchester, thankful that the train service was near back to normal. His dad was waiting when he arrived at Piccadilly Station and, after an awkward greeting, set off back to Worsthorne. The greeting with his mum was much more emotional, with lots of tears and ending the embrace that was difficult for both.

David filled Oliver in with all the details of the abduction of Jackie, ending with a slightly more optimistic statement that they think she is still alive and also saying that the police had no idea regarding the motive for the abduction. Then, right on cue, the phone rang. Sarah nearly fainted on the spot as she held the phone to her ear and heard Jackie whisper,

"Mum, don't worry, I am okay. The headline news today is the massive volcanic eruption in Indonesia."

The sound of the one o'clock news was playing in the background before the phone went dead. David immediately contacted Detective Constable Peterson.

12

Abduction or adoption?

Jackie arose from the chair as the key was turned in the locked door to see Lady Greenway enter, smiling and looking demure in her white chiffon dress.

"How are you feeling today, my dear?"

Jackie scowled with contempt at her kidnapper and replied, "What the devil am I doing here? It is the sixth day you have had me imprisoned. What is your game?"

"Now, now, my dear, this is no way to start our friendship!"

"Stop calling me dear, I am not your dear, lady or no lady, and you are certainly no friend."

Lady Greenway beckoned Jackie to sit down. "We need a little chat."

For the next hour, Lady Greenway explained to Jackie that she had not abducted her but more like adopted her. Jackie listened wide-eyed at the preposterous reason for her abduction. Lady Greenway told her that she loved children and had always craved a daughter of her own. Since her husband died and their clothing empire had collapsed, she had been in danger of losing everything and was heading for bankruptcy. On top of this calamitous situation, she had also received news from the IVF clinic that she could not bear a child.

"What was one to do in such a desperate situation but do my utmost to cling to the only thing I had left, this lovely home and the lifestyle that went with it? However, that was not enough. I needed someone to share it with, and you are that someone." She said that Jackie was just the right age. A young child would be too much to handle in her present circumstances.

"Jackie, I am offering you a life you could only dream about. I am very wealthy, and I want you to share it."

"So where did your wealth come from then?" asked Jackie.

"We shall not go into that now," replied her Ladyship.

"And, if I refuse to comply with your silly plan, what then?"

"You would be foolish to refuse such luxury. Besides, that is not the only thing you would lose, and yes, I know all about Oliver."

Jackie felt herself go pale, slowly realising the many connections to the criminal world this evil woman had.

13

Jackie's contact with Mum and Dad

That morning, Lady Greenway allowed Jackie to join her in the dining hall.

"Today, Jackie, I want you to contact your parents."

Jackie looked at her Ladyship suspiciously and asked her how.

"Obviously, I can't let your parents know your whereabouts at this stage, so I want you to record a message. This will be sent indirectly through one of my contacts."

Jackie wasn't so sure of the motive for this latest twist in the schemes of this crazy woman, but on giving it some thought, agreed. At least Mum and Dad would know she was alive.

The recording, along with the BBC one o'clock news, played simultaneously with Jackie repeating the headline news bulletin to prove it was genuine, which was immediately emailed to a contact in Norwich who sent the recorded message via a public call box. Jackie felt a mixture of relief and anger at having to record the message and was now desperately worried about what her family was going through. Turning to Lady

Greenway she screamed,

"I will never forgive you for what you have put my family through," and howling with grief and anger stormed out of the dining room and returned to her room.

Later in the afternoon, Lady Greenway popped her head around Jackie's door and, with a forced conciliatory smile, asked if she would like to visit the shopping mall in the town. Jackie could not believe her ears, but as her mind immediately turned to an opportunity to escape the clutches of her jailer, she remembered the threat regarding her brother. Her mind was working overtime now and after a long pause answered,

"Yes, thank you, I would like that very much."

At least, thought Jackie, she would have some idea where in the country she was being held.

The chauffeur-driven car pulled up outside the front entrance, and both Jackie and her ladyship climbed into the spacious back seat of the Silver Ghost Rolls Royce. The chauffeur then secured the car doors and proceeded to make his way down the drive and, after twenty minutes, was about to join the M5 when her Ladyship's phone rang.

"The parcel has arrived, your Ladyship."

Lady Greenway tapped on the dividing glass panel and indicated to the chauffeur to stop. Outside the car, the chauffeur and her Ladyship engaged in a conversation, and getting back in the car, her Ladyship informed Jackie that there would be no shopping trip today. Somewhere in a secluded patch of waste ground beside a country lane, the car came to a stop. Another car was already waiting. After exchanging words, a large package was transferred to the boot of the Rolls Royce, after which both cars went their separate ways.

"Who was that, Father Christmas?" asked Jackie, not expecting an answer.

"Oh, just a friend," replied Lady Greenway.

The chauffeur then drove them back to Greenway Mansions.

Back in Worsthorne, Detective Constable Peterson joined David, Sarah, and Oliver at Sarah's home an hour after hearing of the phone call from Norwich. Peterson had already contacted Norwich Constabulary to make some inquiries in the vicinity of the traced public phone box. Peterson was not very optimistic that the investigation in Norwich would produce any positive results.

"We are dealing with a network of criminals that seem to have connections throughout the country, and my guess is that our mystery lady is behind it all. The question is why an innocent seventeen-year-old girl has been abducted. We can assume that the mystery woman in question is involved in drug trafficking, and we can also assume that Jackie may be being groomed to be a drug runner, but I have my doubts about that. There must be another reason."

The reaction to Peterson's comments was met with a mixture of utter despair and deep gloom. After a long silence, David said,

"Where do we start searching for Jackie? It seems an impossible task."

Peterson tried to encourage them all by saying they had ways and means.

"I plan to continue our search where it all began, here in Burnley. Contacts in the drug trafficking trade are our main line of investigation. Two of the most significant drug runners are dead. Contacting their associates is now a priority."

14

A delayed Christmas

Lady Greenway planned to catch up on some last-minute Christmas shopping and intended to take Jackie along with her, whether she liked it or not.

"Jackie, today we are travelling to Exeter to do some shopping and catch up on our delayed Christmas."

Jackie remembered the threat to her brother and knowing that protesting was useless, complied with her Ladyship's demand to cooperate with her sadistic wishes.

The Exeter shopping mall was packed with shoppers. Jackie tagged behind her Ladyship showing little enthusiasm for the whole charade.

"Come along, my dear," said Lady Greenway trying her best to be patient.

Entering a rather expensive-looking clothes shop, Lady Greenway began to sift through racks of gowns. Gathering two or three of the gowns together, she pushed Jackie into the changing room. Jackie refused to be pushed, prompting Lady Greenway to give her a scowl and whisper in her ear,

"Cooperate or else!"

For the rest of the afternoon, shoes, coats, lingerie, and jewellery were bought for Jackie with no expense spared. Back at Greenway Mansions, Jackie was subjected to a fashion parade, with Lady Greenway howling with delight at every change of clothing.

"Today, Jackie, is just the beginning, and in time you will learn to appreciate how lucky you are. We will have the best Christmas meal tonight that you have ever tasted in your miserable life."

From that moment, Jackie decided to go along with her Ladyship's fantasies but was determined not to succumb to this evil woman's brainwashing techniques; Mum, Dad and her brother would never be far from her thoughts.

15

A promising lead

Chief Constable Peterson wished Chief Inspector Braddock was back on duty to offer advice but would have to wait until the New Year. Peterson was reluctant to contact Braddock as he deserved a break to have time with his disabled wife, suffering from multiple sclerosis. Peterson spent hours that day sifting through the data record of convicted drug pushers and suppliers. Most of them were already in jail, but a couple looked promising. Shaun Kennedy and Bill Brighouse had a long history of drug dealing and had only recently been before the bench but had been acquitted on a technicality.

Peterson, equipped with mugshots of Kennedy and Brighouse, spent the evening in the popular drinking dens of Burnley. He got a bit tired of the taste of mineral water and began indulging in the occasional glass of lager. By 11 pm that evening, he had met with little success in his search for the two elusive men and, feeling a little worse for wear through too much lager, decided to go home and try again tomorrow. However, turning down a back street on his way for a taxi, he came across the Flamingo Nightclub and, after permission granted by the bouncer to enter, found a seat in the corner of the nightclub lounge where karaoke was in full session.

Peterson wasn't impressed by the participant who sang like a strangled canary. Surveying the room for any sign of Kennedy and Brighouse was not easy, and he was about to call it a day when the embarrassed singing turn was dragged off and replaced by another male hopeful. Peterson sat up and reached into his inside pocket for his mugshots, and bingo it was Kennedy who was now singing the Beatles song, 'Hey Jude.'

At about 2 am, Peterson stood by the cloakroom as a staggering Kennedy turned up to retrieve his coat.

"Hello, Shaun!"

"Who are you?" muttered Kennedy.

"Just a friend, mind if I join you on your way home?" replied Peterson. "We can share a taxi."

When Peterson promised to pay, Kennedy, who was quite unsteady on his feet, agreed. Kennedy had already booked the taxi earlier in the evening, and when the cab turned up, Peterson thought it unusual to be climbing into an upmarket Range Rover with a fancy number plate. Not much was said during the short journey to Brierfield. Kennedy had just about remembered the address he had given to the taxi driver, much to Peterson's satisfaction. Having dropped Kennedy off, the taxi driver drove Peterson back to his flat, the policeman happy with the outcome of his ongoing investigation. Tomorrow, Shaun Kennedy would receive a visit from his taxi fare benefactor.

16

Another false hope

That morning, Peterson dragged himself out of bed, had a quick breakfast and made his way to his office. He was a bit later than usual, but after only four hours of sleep, getting to the office was a feat in itself. He decided that the first job on his agenda was to ring David and Sarah and update them on his progress.

"Hello David, Matt here."

David was now all ears hoping for some good news.

"Hi Matt, how is the investigation going?"

Peterson realised that what he had to tell David would not exactly have him jumping with joy.

"Early stages yet, David; I have managed to locate a drug pusher that might be a matter of interest, but don't build your hopes up just yet." Peterson heard David give a deep sigh. "Tell you what, how about joining me today? I have located exactly where our drug pusher lives and intend to visit him this afternoon."

David thought the suggestion was a great idea, unconventional perhaps, but he already realised that Peterson wasn't the normal, conventional policeman.

David was worried about Sarah, who, until recently, had been taking the abduction of Jackie relatively well but now she was becoming more and more depressed through lack of sleep and anxiety and because Oliver had returned to Durham. She had no breakfast again that morning. David did what he could to keep her positive, and when he shared Peterson's news, she gave a weak smile and hoped all would go well on their visit to Brierfield and, clinging tightly to him, told him to take care.

Peterson already had the squad car waiting when David arrived at the police station. On the way to visit Kennedy, Peterson briefed David about the night before, apologised for the intermittent yawning and asked David to give him a nudge if he fell asleep.

There was no doorbell to ring on the terraced house tucked down a side street, not even a knocker. Peterson knocked hard on the front door and received no response and, after trying for five minutes or so, heard David call from around the back of the building. Peterson joined him to find the back door wide open. He told David to remain outside while he went in. Having thoroughly searched downstairs, he examined the bedrooms, and it was not long before he found Kennedy's lifeless body on the floor at the side of the bed. He had died from stab wounds. The house was now a crime scene. Unfortunately, Peterson had to inform Chief Inspector Braddock, who was now very much involved in what had become a murder investigation.

By the time Peterson and David arrived back at the police station, they were both in total shock and wondering where they could go from there. Peterson suggested that David return home and join him in the morning; for the rest of the day, he would be busy updating Chief Inspector Braddock on what had transpired so far in this complex case. Braddock wasn't too pleased with having to deal with the three deaths that had occurred so far and wondered where all this would end.

It was midnight when Peterson climbed into bed. The banging of fireworks reminded him that he had just entered 2023, having totally forgotten what day it was. He was about to fall into a very welcome sleep when he suddenly remembered the taxi. For the next hour, he tossed about, his mind racing, trying to remember the number plate on the Range Rover realising that it wasn't a taxi at all. The driver had purposely kept a low profile; the Covid mask and peaked cap hiding most of his face, obviously intentional. Peterson had been too affected by the lager to notice important details of the drive and wished he had stuck to mineral water. Thinking hard and wide awake, he remembered the colour was a maroon-type red with the letters ROD on the number plate. Tomorrow, despite being New Year's Day, would be another busy day pursuing this important lead. Peterson finally succumbed to much-needed sleep.

17

A surprising gift for Jackie

"Happy New Year, my dear!"

Jackie opened her eyes to be greeted by her Ladyship standing at the foot of her bed. Jackie's response was to bury her head under the bedclothes and ignore the unwelcome disturbance.

"You will be interested to know that your brother Oliver is now back in Durham, having spent a couple of days with your mum and dad."

Jackie sat up with a bolt. "How did you know that?" she gasped.

"Never mind that just get up, dear. Your breakfast is waiting for you."

Jackie took her time eating her poached eggs on toast, doing her best to annoy her Ladyship. But nothing she did seemed to annoy her, and Jackie had to admire the woman's patience.

"When you have finished breakfast, my dear, I have a surprise for you."

Jackie looked puzzled and wondered whether it would be good or bad. She took her time drinking her coffee, trying to delay the inevitable, and finally, replacing her empty cup on its saucer, asked,

"So, what's this surprise then?"

"I thought you would never ask," replied her Ladyship. "Look out of the window; I have bought you a New Year present."

Jackie walked over to the large bay window; she could only see a car that wasn't there the night before.

"That Ford Puma is yours, my dear, and here are the keys."

Jackie had been having driving lessons before her abduction and already passed her driving test. Lady Greenway arranged for her to have some tuition under the supervision of her chauffeur. She was unaware that Jackie was already proficient in driving skills, information that Jackie would keep to herself for the moment. Her mind was working overtime now, wondering whether, at some future date, the car might be her means of escape. Her Ladyship so wanted Jackie's appreciation and, putting her hand on her shoulder, asked,

"So, Jackie, do you like your surprise?"

Jackie felt a slight touch of compassion for her Ladyship and began to realise how lonely and unloved this woman was and surprised herself by answering,

"Yes, your Ladyship. It is a very generous gift. Thank you."

18

Oliver's New Year inebriations

Oliver was sorry to have left his mum and dad in the present circumstances but was glad to be back among his friends. The New Year festivities the night before had helped to take his mind off the worry of his missing sister. He had already phoned his mum and dad to wish them a happier outcome to the new year, despite the turmoil they were going through, and promised to keep in touch every day. The truth was that Oliver felt so useless, unable to do anything, and being in Durham would help to blot out the anguish he felt for the plight of his dear sister.

A knock sounded on his flat door and Oliver was glad to see it was Barry, especially as Barry had not been at the party the night before. Barry hugged Oliver and asked for any news on his sister's whereabouts.

"We have received a phone message from Jackie, so we know she is still alive, but further than that, we have no idea where she is or why she has been abducted," he said.

"That's better news," replied Barry, and was surprised to hear himself say, "We need to continue praying for her."

Oliver himself was surprised to hear Barry's remark and answered,

"Er, yes, Barry, we do. Anyway, we need to decide where we are going tonight. I made my New Year's resolution last night and intend to keep it."

"And what was that?" asked Barry.

"Eat, drink, and enjoy myself," replied Oliver forcing an uneasy smile.

Later that evening, Oliver was enjoying the night out with his friends at the Studio club. There was lots of live entertainment, and the help of a few lagers put Oliver in a relaxed mood. On the other hand, Barry was drinking fresh orange juice and appeared much more subdued. As the evening wore on, Oliver's mood began to change. The alcohol was having a detrimental effect on his behaviour, making him more and more erratic. Barry was doing his utmost to persuade Oliver to curb his drinking but to no avail.

The effects of the alcohol set Oliver off shouting loudly, using language which surprised and alarmed Barry, who then tried to help his friend off his seat and lead him towards the toilet to try and calm him down. Staggering to the toilet, Oliver knocked a table flying and splashed drink on a group of young lads; they were not too pleased. One of the group started to swing his fists, knocking Oliver over an adjoining table, causing more mayhem. The intervention of the club staff prevented Oliver from suffering further beatings, and he was quickly led to the exit and ejected from the premises.

Barry managed to get Oliver back on his feet and,

with great difficulty and the aid of a passing stranger, helped him reach his flat, which was, thankfully, not too far away. Barry thanked his helper and, as the stranger disappeared down an alley, he shouted,

"Tell Oliver his sister Jackie is alive and well."

The following morning, Barry called on Oliver to see if he was okay. Oliver was still in bed, and after taking ten minutes to come around, he let his friend in. Barry was alarmed to see his friend's right eye was black and blue and half closed. His lip was swollen, but apart from these facial injuries, he was okay and even managed a smile.

"Well! There is one bit of good news coming from last night's fiasco," said Barry.

"And what's that?" asked Oliver.

"Your sister Jackie is alive and well."

Barry then described the surprising encounter with the stranger who turned up from nowhere and vanished into the night. Oliver did not hesitate to phone his mum describing the events of the previous night, concluding with the comment made by the passing stranger.

"How strange," responded Sarah, and after telling Oliver to get medical attention for facial injuries, she shared the strange encounter with David when he returned from his walk.

19

Another abduction

David and Sarah had spent the previous day quietly but happily together. David was hoping their marriage could eventually be salvaged but knew he had to be sensitive to Sarah's feelings and that much trust would have to be built up before there was a full reconciliation. The arrangements for David's stay were not ideal, but the sofa would suffice for now. Sarah had already put the washer on and done some baking, trying to keep herself busy. Later, David went for his morning stroll in the crisp morning air, thankful that the snow had almost gone. On his return, Sarah could not wait to share news of the phone call she had just received from Oliver. That does sound strange, he thought and contacted Peterson right away.

Peterson was already in his office when he received the phone call from David informing him of his son Oliver's experience with the passing stranger. When Chief Inspector Braddock arrived, Peterson informed him of the latest developments on Jackie's abduction. Braddock agreed that the encounter with a total stranger having personal information was significant and suggested that Peterson take a trip to Durham and, with the cooperation of the Durham constabulary, try and see if he could glean some further knowledge on this latest development. Braddock acknowledged that it was a long shot, but as there was not much else going on at the station, Peterson's absence would not put too much of a strain on the rest of the schedule.

"Two days only, Peterson," called out Braddock.

Having picked up his travelling bag, Peterson decided to call on David and Sarah before embarking on his journey to Durham. As he expected, David asked if he could join him. Sarah wasn't too keen on the idea, but when Peterson suggested she come along too, she reluctantly agreed. Peterson suggested that the couple take a mini holiday in Durham. That way, they could be on hand for Peterson to share any information he might discover. It took David and Sarah twenty minutes to pack a few things for their unexpected break, and Peterson was soon driving north with David and Sarah in the back seat.

They thanked Peterson for the journey and booked a couple of nights at the Holiday Inn Express in Durham. Peterson drove on to his mother's home, which was a lovely surprise for her.

"Matthew! Lovely to see you," greeted his widowed mum.

"Just two nights stay mum, police business, I'm afraid."

Having caught up on the family news and a welcome afternoon tea, Peterson met up with David. Sarah had decided to rest for the evening, wishing them both well on their quest to find more information to help find Jackie. She was hoping that she could spend tomorrow with Oliver and perhaps see some of the sights of this beautiful city.

The first port of call for Peterson and David was to call on Oliver. Climbing the steps to the third floor, they hoped to find him still in his flat as it was early evening. A knock on the door resulted in no response, and assuming Oliver was out, they were about to descend the stairs when Barry came bounding up the steps.

"Just received a text message from Oliver; he's been kidnapped."

David shrieked with horror and almost fell down the stairs. Peterson tried calming the situation and asked Barry what the text said. Barry fumbled for his phone and read out the message,

"I have been bundled into the boot of a car by two men, and I have no idea where they are taking me."

"Is that it?" asked Peterson.

"That's it," replied Barry.

"I need to hold on to your phone for now in case there are any more messages," said Peterson, promising to return it to Barry.

"No need to worry about returning it now, just find Oliver," pleaded Barry.

David had no choice but to return to the Holiday Inn and let Sarah know the bad news, and to be there to support her; the evening was going to be challenging for both. Peterson spent the rest of the evening visiting the various pubs and clubs in the student area, spending most of his time in the Studio club. By midnight, he had drawn a blank in his inquiries and decided to call it a day and resume his investigation the next day.

20

A surprise message to Jackie from Oliver

Jackie spent the morning sitting in her latest acquisition from Lady Greenway. She felt rather overwhelmed by the lavishness of the gift and could not believe that the Blazer blue Ford Puma was hers, but then looking at the registration document noticed it was registered to a name and address in Cardiff, Wales. The car was either stolen or had been registered in a fictitious name and address.

On questioning her Ladyship about the registration document, Lady Greenway assured her that the car did belong to Lady Greenway but now belonged to Jackie. She went on to explain that she could not register the car in Jackie's name until she fully committed herself to accepting her Ladyship as her foster mum and acknowledged that it would take time.

"In time, Jackie, you will forget your parents and learn to like me and, hopefully, one day love me."

Jackie shook her head, amazed at such a ludicrous notion but kept her thoughts to herself. Jackie would go along with her Ladyship's delusion for now, hoping the time would come to escape the clutches of this pathetic, misguided specimen of humanity.

"By the way, Jackie, I would like to show you a video directly after lunch; you will find it most informative."

The butler already had the viewing equipment set up when her Ladyship and Jackie sat together on the large sofa.

"Start the ball rolling, James," instructed her Ladyship.

Jackie gasped in horror as the bruised face of Oliver appeared on the screen. "What have you done to him?" she screamed.

"Oh! Don't worry, dear; he obtained those bruises in a drunken brawl. We helped get him home to his flat."

Just then, Oliver began to speak.

"Love you, Jackie. I have been instructed to tell you to comply with her Ladyship's wishes. I just want to say…"

The video ended abruptly.

"Sorry, Jackie, that is all for now." Her Ladyship dismissed the Butler and, turning to Jackie, said, "We will let your brother go tomorrow. The incident is to let you know how vulnerable your family is if you ever thought of driving off in that car of yours. You are here to stay, so make the most of your good fortune."

21

Anxious times for Oliver's safety

Peterson had already finished breakfast when his mobile rang. David was anxious to know if he had succeeded in his search for Oliver.

"Nothing yet, David. My first port of call today is to visit Oliver's flat and see if there is anything there that can throw some light on the investigation. It's a long shot, but we are working in the dark, and just now, I am not very hopeful."

There was a long pause before David asked if he could meet up at his son's flat.

"Sure, David, meet you there in about an hour."

When they met at Oliver's apartment block, Barry was already sitting on the stair landing, looking as though he had not slept all night. David was pleased but surprised to see him,

"Barry!" What are you doing here?"

"Same as you, hoping Oliver would come through that door," he nodded his head in acknowledgement; words were meaningless just now.

Peterson asked the rest of the group to remain outside the flat as he peered into Oliver's room and was just about to shut the door to avoid contamination when Barry's phone rang.

"Is that Barry?"

Peterson thought it wise to reply 'Yes'. The voice on the other end of the phone continued,

"Listen carefully; your friend Oliver is down a side road next to Milburngate Bridge. He has instructions to wait for you."

Nothing else was said. Peterson ran onto the landing and, dashing down the stairs, called out to the rest of the group,

"Follow me! We are off to find Oliver."

David gasped with relief when they found Oliver sitting by the river looking dishevelled, bewildered, forlorn, and shivering with the cold. Oliver could not believe seeing his dad and Barry and thought he was dreaming. David quickly put an assuring arm around him, saying tenderly,

"Come on, lad, let's get you back to your flat."

Peterson had many questions to ask Oliver but gave him time to adjust to what must have been a very trying experience. On the way to the flat, they called to pick up Sarah, who was soon sitting in the back seat beside Oliver, cradling him in her arms.

Chief Inspector Dolby of Durham CID was informed of the latest developments by Peterson regarding Oliver's abduction and already had a team making inquiries in and around Durham. Oliver's flat was now sealed off as a crime scene. Fingerprints and any traces of DNA were the priority, but Peterson knew that there was a very slim chance of that as this criminal gang was far too sophisticated to leave any evidence of their activities behind. Checking CC cameras in the area of the kidnapping would take many days before it brought any results. In the meantime, Oliver, accompanied by Peterson, was asked to call in at Durham Police Station to give his account of the abduction.

"Sit down, Oliver," beckoned Dolby. "I want you to try and describe the events of your abduction; any small detail will help."

At the end of the session, there was very little information forthcoming from Oliver. He described how they wore gloves and had masked faces, and he was not even able to describe the car or its number. He did, however, hear one of the gang mention 'her Ladyship' to one of his gang members. He also mentioned the fact that they insisted he used his own phone to contact Barry, which resulted in another dead end in tracing Oliver's abductors.

Dolby did suggest that they could arrange to give Oliver a new identity and remove him to another part of the country, but that suggestion was dismissed out of hand by Oliver, and his mum and dad were not over-enthusiastic about the idea either. Dolby assured the family that Oliver's abductors would not succeed a second time without disclosing how he intended to fulfil his plan of protection.

David and Sarah's time to leave Oliver and return to Burnley was heart-breaking but necessary as Oliver insisted on staying to complete his studies. They, too, had to resume a normal life. David had his dental practice to maintain, and Sarah was due for her first shift of the New Year at Burnley General Hospital.

Back at the station in Burnley, Peterson was already researching all the names of Lords and Ladies recorded in the UK, which wasn't easy, especially as no register of manorial lordships was maintained. Peterson also learned that you could buy a Lordship, which added to the confusion. If he were going to get anywhere with this line of investigation, he would have to contact all the UK Police Forces, of which there are over fifty.

Chief Inspector Braddock wasn't happy with the time Peterson was spending on Jackie's abduction case, as other cases were pending, especially cases of domestic violence, which was always a problem at this time of the year. Peterson would have to do most of his research on Jackie's case in his own free time.

22

Jackie's compliance

The strain of worry over Jackie was taking its toll on David and Sarah's hopeful reconciliation. Sarah had to take time off work as the stress of it all was causing bouts of depression. The occasional recorded message from Jackie helped a little, but finding Jackie seemed no nearer than when she was originally abducted.

Oliver was progressing with his studies and hoped to join his mum and dad over Easter. Barry had started attending a local Baptist church in Durham, much to Oliver's disapproval. However, they continued their friendship as Oliver was very inquisitive about why his friend had changed and hoped it was just a passing phase.

David and Peterson met up occasionally, but these meetings were becoming less frequent due to the lack of progress on the case. Meanwhile, in Somerset, Lady Greenway continued lavishing gifts and money on her reluctant adopted daughter. Jackie was trying hard to fight against Lady Greenway's brainwashing but was finding her luxury lifestyle difficult to resist as now there was a bond forming between her and her Ladyship, more out of Jackie's sympathy for this childless and unhappy benefactor.

Jackie was becoming much more concerned about

her mum and dad due to the worry and stress that they must be suffering and insisted that the contact by recorded phone messages should continue at least once a week, but her Ladyship refused her request and suggested once a month would be sufficient much to Jackie's displeasure but felt that she had no other choice due to the impending threat of harm to her brother. However, she had not given up hope of one day returning to Burnley and resuming her normal life. In the meantime, she would go along with Lady Greenway's wishes and try and make the most of the luxury lifestyle she could only dream of in the backwoods of Burnley.

Lady Greenway began to allow Jackie much more freedom, even permitting her to drive her Ford Puma, which was fitted with a tracking device. Jackie had to return at a predetermined time, and if she failed to do so, her brother would suffer the consequences. Lady Greenway always apologised for imposing these restrictions and hoped the day would come when they could be removed altogether. However, Jackie was glad of the limited freedom and aimed to please her Ladyship with subtle acquiescence and compliance with her wishes.

Today, Jackie would surprise her Ladyship with a bombshell. She joined Lady Greenway for breakfast, it was Good Friday, and the sun was shining through the bay window.

"Hello dear, how is my girl this Easter morning?"

"I'm fine, Mum, thank you."

Jackie then bent over her Ladyship and kissed her on her forehead. Lady Greenway was totally shocked and burst out crying.

"My dear Jackie, thank you for a greeting I waited so long for," unable to control her emotions, Lady Greenway rose from her chair and flung her arms around Jackie, crying and sobbing on her shoulder.

"Happy Easter, Mum," responded Jackie with very mixed emotions.

For Jackie, each day brought more treats and fewer restrictions. She had to exercise a lot of self-discipline and remind herself each day of her real self and that the life she was living was an illusion. Writing in her diary each day, the first thing she wrote was, 'My Mum and Dad love me and want me home.' Events of the previous day were then written in minute detail. On finishing her daily record, she concealed the diary under the mattress.

Showing affection for her Ladyship was difficult, to begin with, but as time went on, the relationship progressed in a way Jackie was happy with. The time would come when Lady Greenway's guard would hopefully come down and reveal more of her personal life, information that Jackie would use to her own advantage and nearer to the day when she would make her escape. Today, important friends of her Ladyship would be coming for dinner and Jackie would have to have her wits about her if she was going to convince them that she was very happy and a dutiful, contented, adopted daughter at the behest of her fake mother.

Lady Greenway pulled out all the stops to make the dinner successful. The lavishness of the occasion was all geared to impress some very important VIPs. Apparently, these dinner parties frequently happened as just one more cover-up to hide Lady Greenway's life of drug smuggling and supply to the many cartels up and down the country.

Jackie had been given every beauty facility provided by Lady Greenwood, no expense spared. She received attention to her hair she had never imagined possible. The emeralds in the tiara sparkled as she gazed at herself in the long mirror. The matching earrings, bracelet, and long, flowing gown complimented her dark hair, and Jackie had to pinch herself to make sure the image in the mirror was really her.

There were gasps from the assembly below as she made her way down the long winding staircase to be introduced to Lady Greenwood's guests. The party was soon in full swing with the wine flowing, music playing, and dancing to the accompaniment of a musical quartet which included a very accomplished lady vocalist. Young men were falling over themselves for the privilege of having the next dance with the most beautiful Belle of the Ball.

At the end of a very interesting evening, Jackie lay her head on her pillow, wondering what Lady Greenwood had in store for her next. She would need all her wits and willpower if she were to remain focused on her long-term plan to escape the clutches of her deluded adopted mother.

23

A vital clue

Jackie greeted her Ladyship with her usual morning kiss the next morning and thanked her for a wonderful evening. Lady Greenwood was in a very good mood and could not stop talking about the many compliments received from last night's guests. Many of the young men had left their calling cards for Jackie, not that they would be successful in wooing her, her Ladyship would soon put a stop to that. During the breakfast conversation, Jackie asked her Ladyship if it would be possible to include some personal information in her monthly recorded call to her parents.

"You have a new mum now, Jackie. It would be better to let go of your past and look to a very prosperous and happy future here with me," replied Lady Greenway.

"That is what I intend to do, Mum, but I would like to make sure they are not fretting at home."

"Oh! As you wish, Jackie."

Jackie returned to her room before her Ladyship changed her mind thinking hard to see if she could slip some clue into the phone message that would reveal her location.

Lady Greenway had the recording system all set up when Jackie entered the office. She greeted her

Ladyship with a kiss and sat down, ready to record her message to her mum and dad. Jackie surreptitiously surveyed her surroundings, noticing particularly a large filing cabinet in the corner with the key to the drawer still hanging from the lock. Interesting, thought Jackie, I wonder what secrets are concealed in there. The butler gave Jackie a nudge,

"Are you ready to record your message?"

"Yes!" she replied.

The television was on, and 'Bargain Hunt' was just about to finish a couple of minutes before the start of the 1 o'clock News. Jackie began her message just as the newscaster gave out the headlines.

"Hi, Mum and Dad, this is Jackie. I am very well, so please don't worry. To prove it is me speaking, the teddy you bought me as a child, which is in my bedroom, is called Jasper. Also, the holiday we had when I was ten years old was in Scarborough…"

The butler abruptly terminated the message and downloaded it to one of her Ladyships contacts. Jackie turned to her Ladyship and said,

"Thank you, Mum; I don't think I need to send any more messages. You are quite right; I need to burn my bridges and accept that the life you have offered me is too good to refuse, especially your love and care."

Lady Greenway smiled, "Come, my dear. Let us enjoy the rest of the day."

Back at Worsthorne, Sarah was trying very hard to

make the most of her day; Jackie, however, was never far from her thoughts. It was weeks ago since she had visited the hair salon or even done any serious shopping. All her work colleagues were worried about her mental health, and on the advice of the ward sister, she was taking some time off. She nearly missed the phone call over the noise of the vacuum cleaner, and the moment she heard the ringtone on her mobile, she frantically swiped the phone for contact. Unfortunately, the ringing stopped as she was about to answer the call. Dialling 121, she screamed in frustration on hearing 'the caller withheld their number.'

Sarah sank down on the sofa, wondering whether she had missed a vital phone call from Jackie's abductors. This was a regular occurrence for Sarah; whenever the phone rang, her hopes rose only to be dashed when anyone else rang. The cold callers were the worst calls setting in motion a screaming down the phone to get off the line. Her will to resume vacuuming the lounge had now evaporated, and continuing seemed pointless. As she closed her eyes, trying hard to shut out the world, the doorbell rang. Sarah dragged herself to her feet.

"David!" she cried and flung herself into his arms.

They remained locked together for some time when her mobile rang again.

"You have a message from your daughter, so listen carefully, as it will not be repeated."

"Hi, Mum and Dad, this is Jackie. I am very well, so

please don't worry. To prove it is me speaking, the teddy you bought me as a child, which is in my bedroom, is called Jasper. Also, the holiday we had when I was ten years old was in Scarborough…"

Having the speaker active on the phone allowed David to hear the message, which gave them both a sense of relief, especially at the mention of Jasper, her favourite teddy. However, Sarah began to question in her mind why Jackie was sounding so content and even happy. David put his arm around her, and both sat on the sofa and analysed the latest message together. David sat up with a start,

"We have never been on holiday to Scarborough!"

Sarah looked aghast, "Does that mean it wasn't really Jackie?"

"No! No!" David bawled. "It was Jackie. Don't you see she is trying to tell us something else in that message?"

It then dawned on Sarah that they hired a holiday cottage in Bath, Somerset ten years ago.

"Jackie is somewhere in Somerset and might even be in Bath!"

For the first time in months, Sarah broke out in a huge smile, which then turned into a flood of tears, more relief than sorrow.

Detective Constable Peterson, who was now Detective Sergeant Peterson after a very impressive few months on other cases, was soon joining David and

Sarah at Worsthorne. Sitting down with his welcome cup of coffee, Peterson thanked David and Sarah for their patience regarding the low profile imposed on their case by the Chief Constable,

"I have continued my inquiries in much of my free time, especially trying to get details on Lords and Ladies in England and Wales and will continue to pursue this line of inquiry."

David and Sarah thanked Peterson for his efforts and congratulated him on his promotion.

"So! You tell me you have had another anonymous phone call from Jackie. What exactly was the message?" he asked.

David could hardly contain himself as shared the vital clue.

"Somerset! We suggest you concentrate your search for Jackie in Somerset."

David then recited the whole message in detail and explained that they had never been on holiday to Scarborough and that ten years ago, they hired a self-catering cottage in Bath, Somerset.

"Your daughter is a very clever and brave girl, and what you have just told me will be shared with Chief Inspector Braddock as soon as I return to the station. This may be the break we have been hoping for but don't build your hopes up just yet. Let's just say that the chance of locating your daughter is much more optimistic than it was before this latest communication from her."

Back at the station, Peterson explained the latest developments on Jackie's case to Braddock. A couple of hours later, Braddock called Peterson into his office and told him that he was given a special dispensation to spend a week with Avon and Somerset Constabulary, who would give him every assistance in his search for Jackie.

"They are having lots of drug problems, especially in the Bath area, and would welcome any information that would lead to the organisers of this pernicious and evil trade in drugs. They will also help in locating any nobility in their area. Be very careful and don't take unnecessary risks; these drug pedlars are very dangerous. Any error of judgment could jeopardise not only the safety of Jackie but also her brother Oliver. I suggest you get a good night's sleep to prepare for your long drive to Somerset early in the morning."

Peterson thanked Braddock and promised that he would do his best to find Jackie and, if he were successful, would let him know before he made any attempt to try and contact her. That same evening Peterson rang David and Sarah to let them know the latest developments and promised to keep in touch during his time in Somerset. David and Sarah were now experiencing a mixture of trepidation and excitement. It did enter David's mind as to whether he should ask if he could join Peterson but remembered that he had a heavy schedule at the dental surgery the following day.

24

Jackie tries to stay focused

Last night's visit to the Bristol Old Vic Theatre had been most enjoyable and helped Jackie to forget that she was a kidnap victim. Lady Greenway loved the theatre, and during the drive back to Greenway Mansions, she chatted excitedly about the performing artists' details and the play's dialogue. Jackie was seeing a different side to her which made her feel happy and yet uncomfortable at the same time. In a sense, the whole evening had been a perfect and enjoyable evening.

Her Ladyship continued to chat during a late supper and would have kept Jackie talking for another hour or so. However, Jackie rose from her chair and, kissing Her Ladyship on the cheek, asked if she might be excused as she was feeling rather tired after a very happy day. Her Ladyship held her hand for a while and, with a beaming smile and a squeeze of Jackie's hand, agreed that it was time to call it a day.

As Jackie lay her head on her pillow, an overwhelming feeling to accept the present situation was greater than ever. Fighting off the sleep and feeling of contentment, Jackie retrieved the diary from under the mattress and for the next hour wrote about all the things she could remember relating to home, the names of all her friends, her favourite haunts, the Lancashire countryside where she loved to ramble, Burnley football club of which she was an avid supporter, and the local Baptist church where she was a regular worshipper, anything to take her mind off Greenway Mansions and its luxurious lifestyle and the temptation to surrender her will to a life that had everything except freedom.

25

Barry's friendship with Oliver under strain

Meanwhile, back in Durham, Barry was becoming increasingly concerned over Oliver's erratic behaviour. Drinking to excess was also a major problem, affecting his studies, and missing most of the lectures. Barry regularly called on him in the mornings only to find him still in bed. Today going on for 11.30 am, Barry found Oliver still asleep. He sat at his bedside and waited patiently for him to stir and open his eyes.

"Morning Oliver, would you like some coffee?" he asked gently.

"Oh, it's you, Barry. What time is it?"

"Going on for lunchtime."

"Sorry, Barry, not feeling too well of late. Must get my act together. Things seem to be falling to pieces around me just now."

"Oliver, I think you need some help; you can't face your problems alone. The abduction has had a more serious effect on you than you realise."

"For goodness' sake, don't contact Mum or Dad. I don't want them to start worrying about me on top of their worries over Jackie."

"I have no intention of doing that. Come on, let's call in Costa and have a nice cappuccino," suggested Barry, and after a shower and shave, Oliver joined his best friend for that needy hot drink.

Having found a secluded table and been served their cappuccino and buttered toast, Oliver began to talk as he had never talked before. Barry thought it wise to listen as Oliver tried to explain how he had lost the will to face each new day, and the excess drinking was just a means of dulling the pain, complaining that he didn't even like the stuff.

"I want to finish my course at the university and one day work as a biologist, but I am worried that it's turning into a pipe dream," lamented Oliver.

For the next hour and a couple more coffees, Oliver poured out his worries and anxieties and, turning to his good friend, said,

"Thanks for listening, Barry, I feel a little better having been able to offload my troubles on your sympathetic shoulders."

"Dear Oliver, there are greater shoulders than mine to offload your troubles on."

"And who might that be then?" asked Oliver looking puzzled.

Barry had to summon up all his courage as he answered,

"God!"

"God!" gasped Oliver. "You sound like my sister."

Barry smiled nervously,

"Do you remember those two Nigerian students talking about their faith a couple of months ago? Well, I decided there and then that I needed to know more about the Christian faith. I have always dismissed Christianity as irrelevant but hearing those two guys talking about something they really believed in troubled me for many days, so much so that I decided to try and find some answers at the local Baptist church. I have been attending regularly for a few Sundays now and am becoming more and more convinced in the truth and claims of Christianity."

"Does that mean you have gone all religious, Barry?" asked Oliver frowning.

"It means that my life has a new dimension and meaning. It means that for the first time in my life, I am beginning to understand why we are here. It means that I now know God to be a reality."

"Whoa, Barry! How in the world do you know God to be real? Where is he? I believe in what I can see."

"Perhaps then, when you look again, you might see God in the things surrounding you," replied Barry. "The preacher on Sunday mentioned this in his sermon quoting from a part of the New Testament. I think it might have been one of the letters written by the Apostle Paul. The verse he chose mentioned God's invisible attributes being seen in his creation."

Oliver was now getting more annoyed and, raising his voice, almost screamed, "So, we are to believe in something invisible, that's rubbish, and as far as creation is concerned, it's been proved false by the theory of evolution."

"God is invisible because he is Spirit, and as far as evolution is concerned, I am glad you described it as a theory."

Barry was now wondering whether to pursue the conversation as he thought Oliver was getting too riled but plucking up more courage and praying in his heart for God's help, he decided to throw caution to the wind.

"It also means that the burden and worry of judgement for my godless existence have been placed on the shoulders of a Saviour who loved me and gave his life for me on a wooden cross two thousand years ago. It means that I am not perfect and never will be in this life but now I have the help of a merciful God in overcoming my imperfections, and if you will allow me to use an unpopular word to describe those imperfections, the real term is sin."

"Woah, Barry, I can't take any more of this nonsense. Can a leopard change its spots?"

"No, but God could change its spots if he wanted to, and that is the whole point. Only God can change us, as we can't change ourselves."

"I don't need a prop, Barry. If you need a prop in your life, you are welcome to it."

Oliver was now getting more exasperated, and to Barry's great sadness, he asked him to leave his apartment. Barry then surprised himself by inviting Oliver to the Christian Union meeting at the campus that same evening.

"If your God is as great as you say he is, maybe he will lift me up on a cloud and carry me there, Barry. I don't want anything to do with your religion. I might condescend to see you again someday when you come to realise that you have been brainwashed and radicalised. Your god will have to transport me there as I won't be going of my own accord. Goodbye."

Even as he walked down the stairs, Barry was praying for God to open the heart of Oliver, whose loss of friendship would be hard to bear.

26

Peterson on dangerous ground

Detective Sergeant Peterson arrived in Bath in a very optimistic mood and looked forward to meeting Chief Inspector Rainford of Avon and Somerset Constabulary. His accommodation for the week had all been arranged in the centre of Bath, which seemed a good starting point for his investigation. They had arranged to meet at the Grand Pump Room for informal introductions and a midday lunch. Chief Inspector Rainford was due for retirement in a couple of months.

"Good afternoon, Peterson, my name is Jack Rainford, and I have been asked to help you in your search for Jackie Mitchell; it will probably be my last assignment before I retire. Very sad to hear of this case; let's hope we can locate this poor girl and get her back to her family."

Peterson warmed to Rainford and hoped to learn from his experience and long service in the force.

Peterson's accommodation was basic but suitable, and after an afternoon nap, he decided to find somewhere to have his evening meal. He made his way down Manvers Street, manoeuvering through the hordes of late shoppers and tourists. Deciding to turn down a side street in his search for a quiet meal, he became conscious of being watched by two men on the opposite side of the road. Quickening his pace, his suspicions were confirmed when the men began to follow. He thought it a good idea to go into the nearest shop, which turned out to be a ladies' hairdresser. Rather embarrassed by the surprised looks of customers and staff, he asked one of the staff if they had a back entrance. Not waiting for an answer, he brushed past the lady, knocking her sideways and was just in time to avoid a bullet that embedded itself in the wall where he had been standing just a few seconds earlier.

The sound of screams faded as Peterson hurriedly descended the steps leading to the back street. Running as fast as he had ever done in his entire life, he reached the busy shopping centre and, as soon as he felt relatively safe to do so, rang the police headquarters, telling them to get armed police to the hairdressers in Manver Street right away and also to send a patrol car to pick him up and return him to the police headquarters.

Chief Inspector Rainford arrived at the station a few minutes after Peterson at about 7.30 pm. He found Peterson in a state of shock, drinking strong black coffee and offered his heartfelt condolences for the terrifying experience he had just endured.

"What I would like to know is how anyone knew why I was in Bath. It is obvious that these two men were determined to see an end to me and my investigation." Peterson was now looking intently at Rainford, waiting for an answer.

Rainford slumped in his chair beside his desk and said, "I hate to say this, but the word 'mole' comes to mind. No one knew of your visit outside of this station, and it is either a coincidence or a planned operation that you were nearly killed tonight."

Peterson nodded his head, adding that the tentacles of this drug gang spread much wider than he ever realised.

"However, with your help, I intend to continue my investigation but would appreciate armed assistance as I try to track down this elusive drug baroness."

After a long pause and a look of deep concern, Rainford remained silent, then turned to Peterson and said,

"I will grant you those wishes and give you all the assistance you need. I will also ensure that your movements are known only to me and the armed escort, whom I know I can trust. We first need to transfer you to Taunton Police Station under cover, where you can conduct your inquiries in relative safety."

Within the hour, Peterson was on his way. For the sake of his own security, he could not enlist the help of any of the police staff in his inquiry and he spent the rest of the day at Taunton police headquarters examining a file containing a list of peeresses in the Avon and Somerset area. Countesses, viscountesses, and baronesses were all scrutinised, those who were territorial and those who were non-territorial. The daughters of dukes, marquesses, and earls were also checked over in his search for Jackie's abductor. Having completed his search for prospective titled ladies in the area, he found only two of any interest. He realised from the start that the title 'ladyship' used in Durham could have been referring to her as a mark of respect as the drug gang leader. Tomorrow, however, he would pay a visit along with Rainford's chosen armed officer to the two ladies remaining on the list, if only to eliminate them from his inquiries.

27
John Bland

Specialist protection officer John Bland joined Peterson that same afternoon. Dressed in plain clothes and keeping his firearm well concealed, no one in Taunton Police Headquarters had any inkling of his role. Peterson estimated Bland to be in his forties, a big man and quite an imposing figure, and in Peterson's estimation, slightly overweight.

"My name is Bland, John Bland; I am here to give you a hand in your investigation."

Bland held out his hand, shaking Petersons' hand warmly, if not a little painfully. Peterson could not help quoting in his head, my name is Bond, James Bond, and hoped this chap could emulate Bond's deftness.

The first visit the following morning was to a countess near Glastonbury, who was shocked to have a visit from a policeman. When Peterson mentioned the abduction of a girl, she was quite indignant at the slightest suggestion that she or any of her staff could have anything to do with such a preposterous idea. A call to the butler soon had Peterson led down the drive back to his car, calling out as Peterson drove off,

"Next time you want to see her Ladyship, book an appointment."

From the back seat, Bland muttered, "I assume you

are going to cross her off the list?"

"Far from it," he replied.

The second visit to a Baroness on the outskirts of Bridgewater was much more welcoming. After half an hour and two cups of tea in the presence of the Baroness, it seemed obvious that she knew nothing of a missing girl and even offered to make inquiries among the nobility herself.

"I will inform you of any information gleaned from my friends and not-so-friendly friends. Gossip is a common pastime among the idle rich in this area."

Peterson smiled and thanked her for her hospitality.

"Not at all, my dear, anytime."

"So, any success?" asked Bland.

"The only success was a nice cup of tea and a mince pie. Nothing doing there, I am afraid."

Bland wished he could have had a mince pie and asked where next.

"Back to Glastonbury, we need to do more checking on the unhelpful Countess."

28

Too much for Sarah

In Worsthorne, David was becoming extremely worried about Sarah's mental health. He was back home to be on hand to see to his dental practice, so he could not see her as often as he would have liked. She was still off sick and taking the abduction of Jackie very badly. That same evening David intended to call on her as she sounded desperate during their regular morning phone call. Sarah's front door was locked when David arrived at her home that evening, which seemed strange as she was expecting him. There was no usual greeting when he unlocked the door and entered. Calling her name and receiving no response, he assumed she had gone out for some reason and was about to leave when he noticed her keys on the dining table. David bounded up the stairs and found her lying on the bed, totally unresponsive to David's attempts to wake her up. Two empty paracetamol blister packs lay on the bedroom floor, prompting him to ring 999.

The ambulance arrived within fifteen minutes, which seemed like days to David. The paramedics soon administered acetylcysteine through an intravenous drip and advised that they needed to take her promptly to accident and emergency.

"Is she going to die?" David asked, ashen-faced.

"Try not to worry; you can travel with us where she will get the best medical help needed. You can help by getting her down these steep stairs."

With David's help, the paramedics soon had her in the ambulance and on the way to the hospital with blue lights flashing.

The greatest worry for the medical staff was damage to Sarah's liver, as no one knew how many of the sixteen capsules she had taken or how long she had the paracetamol in her system. David could only estimate the length of time between 9 am that morning and 6 pm in the evening. Anything over eight hours was extremely serious, so it was important to determine when she took the overdose. Sarah was now coming around, but the doctors could not get a coherent answer from her. However, they heard a mumbled, "Why did you not let me die?"

29

Her Ladyship's knowledge alarms Jackie

Jackie enjoyed the momentary freedom of driving around the Somerset countryside. She had been instructed to return to Greenway Mansion by 4 pm, and as she drove onto the drive, a car passed by occupied by two men. Two more drug pedlars thought Jackie and tried her best to read the number plate and, with a mental image of a number displayed in the driving mirror, tried to log it in her memory.

"There you are, my dear, hope you enjoyed your drive," greeted Lady Greenway.

"Yes, Mum, it was nice to see more of this lovely county of Somerset."

Despite her abduction and the trauma Jackie had been through in the last few months, her emotional attachment to Lady Greenway grew stronger, which Jackie was finding difficult to control. Lady Greenway had an endearing and attractive personality and, at times, displayed a vulnerability that Jackie felt hard to resist. In different circumstances, Jackie would have had no difficulty adopting her as her favourite aunt. When the time did come to escape Lady Greenway's clutches, it would not be easy. But, in the meantime, Jackie had to keep focused on escaping from her illusionary and imagined role of motherhood.

"I have some really good news for you, Jackie. According to my friends in Lancashire, your mum was seen laughing and smiling in the Burnley shopping centre this morning."

Jackie did not quite know how to respond to this information but, on instinct, replied with an enthusiastic,

"That's good to know, and now I can relax and enjoy my time with you, Mum. I am going to take a shower now and will join you for dinner later." Jackie kissed her Ladyship on the cheek and returned to her room.

She was far from happy on hearing her Ladyship's 'good news'. The fact that her contacts could identify her mum and probably her dad was deeply worrying. The information itself sounded dubious and for her Ladyship to even mention it made Jackie even more anxious for her mum's welfare. At least it helped Jackie to be even more determined to return to her real mum and dad, whom she loved dearly. She now tried to remember the number plate as seen in the mirror and, after much concentration, wrote it down in her diary.

30

More trouble for Oliver

Oliver was missing his friend Barry as he propped up the bar in the Red Lion. After a couple of lagers, he decided to move on to the club further down the road, which held more promise for girl company. Oliver was not disappointed as there was not only a hen party in full swing but more females looking a bit spare. In normal circumstances, Barry would be a restraining influence on Oliver's unbridled out-of-control behaviour, especially after a drink too many, and by the time it had reached 9 pm, Oliver was well and truly intoxicated. Pushing his way through the throng of young revellers and helping to spill their drinks on the way, he made an unsteady beeline for a blonde-haired girl who had been glancing his way for the past half hour or so.

"Hi! I'm Oliver; why is such a gorgeous girl like you standing all alone in a crowded place like this?"

"Oh! I am just waiting for a handsome hunk like you to turn up; mine is a gin and tonic if you are buying. On second thoughts, there may not be much gin and tonic left in the glass by the time you have been to the bar and back, and I suggest we make our way to my flat for a nice quiet drink and anything else that may be on your mind. By the way, my name is Joyce."

"Pleased to make your acquaintance, I'm Oliver; just lead the way."

As Oliver stumbled along the cobbled street, holding onto Joyce's arm, more for support than affection, a familiar voice rang out from across the street.

"Hi, Oliver!"

Barry was returning from the Christian Union meeting. Oliver pretended he had not heard him and kept his head down.

"Who's your friend?"

"No idea, keep moving," replied Oliver quickening his unsteady pace.

Five minutes later, they arrived at a dingy alley where two men waited in the shadows. Blonde Joyce had now disappeared, and the two thugs soon had Oliver on his back and were rifling through his pockets. They failed in their attempts to rob him of his mobile phone and wallet due to a welcome intervention from Barry, with his fists flying. The two assailants thought it wise to abandon their little scheme and retire to nurse their bruises and in the case of one of them, a bloody nose.

Back at Oliver's flat, Barry had a real struggle to get Oliver up the stairs, but after heaving him on the bed, remained with him throughout the night, concerned that he might choke on his own vomit.

The next morning, Oliver opened his eyes to be met with a smiling Barry standing next to his bed with a mug of coffee.

"Barry! What are you doing here?"

Slowly Oliver began to remember the events of the previous evening. Barry was glad to see that his friend was no worse for his ordeal, and as he left, he called out,

"Your wallet and mobile phone are on the dressing table. I will have to love you and leave you; I have a lecture to attend. See you later."

31

Worries over Sarah's health

Back in Burnley General Hospital, David sat by the bedside of his wife, Sarah, waiting anxiously for any sign of recovery from the drug overdose. After checking the heart monitor and blood pressure, the nurse left, leaving David dozing on and off during his bedside vigil. He was grateful when the hot coffee provided by the drinks trolley attendant arrived. His cup of coffee nearly took off as there came a groan and shout from Sarah as she sat up,

"Where is my daughter, Jackie?"

David was just in time to hold onto her and prevent her from jumping out of bed which would have caused havoc with the medical equipment attached to various parts of her body. The drip stand wobbled but remained upright. David managed to hold on until Sarah realised where she was, and as she slowly reclined back onto the bed, she whispered,

"Sorry!"

It was another half hour before she fully came around, and after a welcome drink of water, David asked her what time had she taken the paracetamol.

"It was during the afternoon. I had just made myself a mug of tea and was feeling like the loneliest person in the world and began asking myself what the point of it all was. I had already taken two capsules for a headache and foolishly swallowed the rest of the remaining capsules amounting to about twelve altogether. I staggered upstairs, lay on the bed and waited for the inevitable. I am so sorry, David."

He held onto her hand and vowed there and then that he would never leave her if that was her wish, to which she replied, "I love you, David, and if I get better, I want you with me always."

A tear rolled down his cheek as he replied, "We will get our beloved daughter back. We must not lose hope."

32

A practice in surveillance

Scrambling through rhododendron bushes, D.S Peterson, with John Bland close behind, paused to peer through his binoculars to take a closer look at the car pulling up outside the entrance to the Countess of Glastonbury's imposing stately home.

"Keep your head down, Bland," Peterson whispered.

Bland's bulky frame was too exposed for Peterson's liking. The unfriendly butler awaited the visitor to escort her up the steps and into the main hall. This was the fifth visitor to arrive that day, and Peterson decided to wait until evening before taking a closer look.

"It's now or never," he said and cautiously crept through the grounds to be as close to the bay window as possible.

Peering through the window, he observed a dozen or so guests gathered around the dining table, all eating and drinking happily. Bland had joined Peterson at the window and was now salivating at the sight of the glorious feast spread across the large table. The appetising odour of the roast venison wafted through the open window, which produced a loud sigh from Bland, causing a couple of heads to turn towards the open window.

"Run!" urged Peterson.

As they bounded across the lawn, they heard the dogs barking which were soon in pursuit of the two intruders. Peterson had already scaled the high-gated entrance whilst Bland was still halfway across the football pitch-sized lawn. Our friendly butler was also running close behind, ordering the dogs to seize their prey. Bland, however, reached his destination just in time, minus a piece out of his trousers. As they climbed into the car with the Butler ranting at the gate, Bland panting and puffing wheezed,

"I must try to visit the gym more often."

The following day, Peterson submitted a full report via the telephone to Chief Inspector Rainford of the investigation so far. Rainford smiled on hearing Bland had lost a piece of his trousers and hoped he was handy with a needle and thread.

"I should continue your surveillance of the Glastonbury residence," advised Rainford, "only try and avoid those nasty dogs next time."

"I certainly will, Chief Inspector. I also intend to call on Lady Greenway at the first opportunity. There are no dogs to worry about there."

Peterson and Bland took up the same position at the Countess of Glastonbury's grounds the next day. Bland had brought three pork pies with him and had already scoffed one of them in the first five minutes of the surveillance.

"We may be here for some time; I suggest you hang on to the other two for later," suggested Peterson.

There were lots of comings and goings at the Glastonbury's but nothing confirming Peterson's suspicions that the investigation on the Countess of Glastonbury was a red herring. Peterson could not believe that Rainford might be the mole and Bland his accomplice but decided to go along with the ruse of letting Rainford think that the Countess of Glastonbury was the chief suspect. As the evening approached, Peterson suggested that he and Bland take up their positions outside the bay window again.

"Keep your head down this time, Bland."

The Countess was entertaining guests again, and as Peterson peered cautiously through the bay window, he noticed the Prime Minister talking to the Countess. Security services would not be far away, thought Peterson, and on the spur of the moment, gave a loud cough and decided to scarper with Bland taken totally by surprise, which slightly delayed his decision to follow suit. Peterson had scaled the gate before Bland had even started to cross the lawn. Looking behind, Peterson was able to catch a glimpse of two policemen rugby-tackling Bland. Poor Bland thought Peterson, his pork pies won't be very eatable now.

Peterson was soon driving down the A361 to Bridgewater, hoping he was not too late to call on Lady Greenway. On the way, he was thinking hard about how to convince her Ladyship of the reason for his unexpected visit. He still had a mental image of the solitary female driver and the car which passed them on the drive on their previous visit. It was approaching 8 o'clock when Peterson finally arrived at Greenway Mansions. Cautiously approaching the main gate, he was surprised to find it wide open and even more surprised that the main front door was also open. Calling out to see if he could receive a response, his call was met with silence.

The whole house was deserted. Peterson went through every room and, entering one, found it to be totally ransacked. The main safe was wide open, and filing cabinets were stripped bare. A further search around the back of the building revealed a couple of saloon cars, one of which was a Ford Puma. Peterson's heart sank as the whole situation began to dawn on him. Lady Greenway, if that was her title and name, had done a runner to who knows where taking Jackie with her.

CI Rainford was fuming when Bland returned to the station accompanied by two Metropolitan police officers.

"Is this yours?" asked one of the officers with a smirk.

"No damage done; have a nice day," with that parting refrain, the officers left the station. Just then, the phone rang; it was Peterson.

"Sorry, Chief Inspector, hope Bland is ok. I will give a full report in the morning. Suffice it to say, for now, our visit to the countess was the proverbial wild goose chase."

Peterson did not mention his visit to Greenway

Mansion, unaware that his movements had been monitored. That same evening, he rang DI Braddock back in Burnley and gave him a full account of his investigation so far.

"I'm afraid we've come to an impasse, sir, and I am at a loss as to where to go from here. This Lady Greenway could be anywhere by now. In view of our suspicions regarding DI Rainford, should we ask him to get the forensics in to go over the Greenway mansion?"

Braddock was silent for a moment before saying,

"We will leave it for now in that way, Rainford will be unaware of your visit. Remain in Somerset for a few more days. Hopefully, something might turn up, and take care."

"I will, sir, and thank you for your support."

33

A new location for Jackie

On the day of Peterson's intention to visit Greenway Mansions, Lady Greenway opened her sleepy eyes as the telephone rang beside her bed. The caller had some bad news that needed to be acted upon immediately. After a quick shower and getting dressed, she made her way to her office accompanied by her butler. Two hours later, she joined Jackie for breakfast, trying hard to look happy.

"Good morning, Jackie!"

Jackie was surprised to be addressed by her name and not 'my dear.' Pouring herself a cup of coffee, her Ladyship continued to smile. "Jackie, I am so happy to have you here. My life had very little meaning before you came along. Please, please, don't ever leave me."

Such an emotional plea took Jackie aback, and rising from her chair; she went across to give her Ladyship a kiss on the cheek and a squeeze of her hand.

"What are our plans today, Mum?"

Lady Greenway smiled and could not wait to reveal her plans,

"I thought we could spend a few days at my summer retreat in Torquay. The weather report for the rest of this month of July is quite favourable."

"That sounds wonderful, Mum. I shall enjoy putting some colour back in my cheeks. Thank you so much; I really don't deserve your love and kindness."

"Nonsense Jackie, what's mine is yours. Just remember we are family now."

Jackie's mind was buzzing with thoughts of what to do before they departed for Torquay. On her way to her room, she heard voices coming from Lady Greenway's office. The door was closed, and the voices were almost inaudible, but Jackie managed to catch details of where they might be staying. She also heard her Ladyship demand,

"Guard that with your life."

Jackie quickly moved along the corridor just in time to conceal herself in her room doorway as the butler left the office carrying a brown briefcase.

They left for Torquay that very morning, followed by the butler driving a Ford Transit.

34

A vital lead for Peterson

Peterson decided to revisit Greenway Mansion before Bland turned up. Realising that Lady Greenway's contacts would return to the mansion to destroy any evidence, he engaged the blue flashing light to save time. Across from the mansion's main entrance, he found some open ground alongside a wooded area that helped conceal the car. The mansion was still deserted when he entered, and bounding up the stairs, he began to search the many rooms. Two rooms were of particular interest as they both contained ladies' clothes and accessories, one of which would have surely been occupied by Jackie, but deciding which one was posing a dilemma for Peterson.

Looking occasionally through the bay window for a sign of any approaching vehicle, he searched closets and drawers for any clues. Forensics will not like this, thought Peterson, but he carried on regardless, turning beds over and scattering clothes in all directions. The first bedroom revealed nothing. Proceeding to the next bedroom and emptying drawers, Peterson found a key ring displaying the Ford logo. The wardrobe was next to be emptied of its contents, followed by removing pillows and bedclothes. Just at that moment, he heard cars pulling up outside the mansion. He was about to make his exit when he saw the exposed diary sticking out from under the mattress and stuffed it inside his shirt.

The back entrance was now the only option, but finding it was proving difficult. After trying many doors, one finally revealed a stairway that led through the kitchen to the welcome open air and the drive. Peterson ran quickly across the back lawn, where he concealed himself in the rhododendron shrubs and remained there until late into the evening.

All was quiet when Peterson emerged from his hiding place and dodging through the undergrowth, he eventually reached the main road and returned to his car, wondering what to do next. He would most certainly have to explain to Rainford where he had been that day. On his return to Taunton Police Station, the desk sergeant informed Peterson that Rainford had phoned and would he please return his call. Settling down by his desk, Peterson rang Rainford and waited for the fireworks.

"Hello, Peterson. Thanks for returning my call. Bland tells me that he turned up at Taunton only to find you had already left. I need to speak with you face to face and suggest we meet at the Premier Inn, Bridgewater Road, about 8 o'clock this evening if that's okay with you?"

"Of course, chief inspector. I also fully understand the need for discretion. See you later."

Peterson realised what a perilous situation he was now in but knew that meeting up with Rainford had to be done. Tomorrow, he would devour the contents of the precious diary still tucked away inside his shirt.

Peterson joined Rainford in the Premier lounge, and after drinks were ordered, Rainford smiled and asked Peterson if he was okay.

"I'm fine, thank you, sir."

"Now, Peterson, this is not an interrogation, but I would like to know the reason for your hasty departure today and whether you found any new leads in your investigation."

"I revisited Greenway mansion today. The reason I didn't wait for Bland is probably due to paranoia. I have got to the state where I am afraid to trust anyone and to be honest, I don't exactly know whether I can trust you."

Rainford looked genuinely surprised at Peterson's reply but, after a pause, asked him if his meeting with Lady Greenway had produced any results.

"No sir, when I arrived at Greenway mansion, there were already two cars outside the entrance. I think they were Range Rovers, and the occupants were armed with handguns. I quickly reversed and retreated down the drive, and, in my panic, I failed to get the registration number of the vehicles."

Rainford's face clouded over, "So why didn't you ring for back up and why did you not let me know?"

"As I said," replied Peterson, "I am not sure whom I can trust. I am fairly sure that this armed gang was tipped off and could have been looking for me. There is one more important thing I need to tell you. In order to cover my back, I have mailed a letter to Chief Inspector Braddock with strict instructions that it must only be opened and read on my demise."

After a shake of the head, Rainford appeared shocked and bewildered as he listened to Peterson and said,

"Working together depends on mutual trust, and it is obvious that that trust has broken down between us. You are at liberty to continue your investigation with Avon and Somerset Constabulary or return to Lancashire. I am due to retire next week, so perhaps you may like to speak with my replacement, Chief Inspector Ralph Slater before you decide. Suffice it to say, I am not the mole."

"I sincerely hope not, Chief Inspector, and I hope you have a happy retirement."

Peterson returned to his flat, unhappy with having to lie and even more confused about Rainford being the mole. Feeling very tired after such an eventful day, Rainford lay on his bed, fully clothed and fell into a deep sleep.

The following morning, feeling much more refreshed, he eagerly took up Jackie's diary and began to scrutinise every page. However, it was the last entry in the diary that really sparked his interest: 'Lady Greenway has decided that we should spend a few days in Torquay; not sure about the exact location but could possibly be Beach Crescent. I will reveal exactly where in Torquay when we get back.'

35

Hope

The sun was shining when Peterson arrived in Torquay, and the first priority was to find somewhere to stay. The back street B&B would do for now, and after he had unpacked, decided to inform David and Sarah of the latest developments.

Sarah was back home after her brief stay in the hospital. She was glad David had suggested staying with her for a few days. The following afternoon David's mobile rang, and for Sarah to hear the call, David put the phone on the speaker; they were thrilled to hear Peterson's welcome voice.

"Hello, David, hope you and Sarah are well."

David confirmed that they were both well and turned toward Sarah smiling.

"I have much to tell you, but the first thing to say is that Jackie is okay. It's a long story, but I have managed to retrieve a diary written by her, and the latest entry informs me that she is in Torquay, which is where I am now. I may have a location that I intend to visit this evening. I will keep you informed of any progress, so keep positive; this may be the lead we have been hoping for."

David and Sarah could not have been happier. David responded by telling Peterson to take care and not to put himself in danger.

David and Sarah hugged each other, and for the first time in many weeks, the gloom began to lift from Sarah's weary shoulders.

36

Sinister developments for Oliver

Leaving his breakfast cereal untouched, Oliver sat reflecting on events in his life in the last few weeks. He was so grateful that his friendship with Barry was still intact despite his disdain for Barry's religious turnaround and change of lifestyle. Oliver promised himself to attend a Christian Union meeting to make amends for his antagonism toward Barry, not that he would ever become religious himself, but he hoped it would show some gratitude for Barry's support at a time when he really needed help.

Oliver would attend his first lecture for a few weeks today and vowed to do less drinking, more studying, and get his life back on track. It was a lovely summer's day; that helped lift Oliver's spirits and put a spring in his step. Across the road, a familiar voice called out; it was Barry. Oliver was just about to cross the road to join his friend when they heard a screech of brakes, and Oliver was bundled into the back of a car that sped off at breakneck speed. A hood placed over his head and a gag around his mouth left Oliver terrified. Nothing was said on the journey, which did not take long before he was manhandled up a flight of stairs and pushed into a room; his hands and feet were securely tied, and the gag remained over his mouth. Oliver heard the key turn in the lock and then came a deathly silence.

Meanwhile, Barry remained stuck to the spot, terrified at what had just taken place in broad daylight on a busy street, but despite his complete shock, he managed to lock the car number securely in his memory, grab a passing student and yank him off his bike peddling furiously in pursuit of the abductor's car.

He lost sight of the car several times but managed to keep on its tail, with the help of traffic lights in his favour. The car turned down a side street and pulled up outside an apartment block where Barry was able to see two men enter the main door taking a hooded Oliver unceremoniously with them. Barry waited at a safe distance and did not have to wait long before the two assailants exited the building and drove off.

Finding Oliver in a ten-storey apartment block would not be easy, but at least he knew he was somewhere in there. Methodically, Barry knocked on every floor door, apologising several times for disturbing the residents. On the seventh floor, with his knuckles already sore, calling out Oliver's name brought forth a faint muffled groan. After several shoulder charges against a very stubborn door, it finally gave way allowing Barry to leap into the room, release a trembling Oliver from his bonds and give him an assuring hug.

David's mobile rang just as he was about to administer the drill in the old lady's mouth. The indicator was telling him that Oliver was calling. David turned off the drill leaving the lady sitting there with her mouth wide open.

"Hello!" the caller on the other end of the line was

not Oliver. "We have your son. Tell your friends to call off the dogs, or he dies."

The phone call ended, leaving David shaking with fear.

"Sorry, Mrs Thompson, but I must leave for an urgent matter."

Mrs Thompson closed her mouth only to open it again to remonstrate with the dental nurse, who was equally annoyed at David's sudden departure.

He made his way to Burnley police station as hastily as possible and asked the desk sergeant if CI Braddock was available. Braddock greeted David and asked him to sit down and tried to calm him down.

"It's my son, he has been kidnapped again, and you are the only one I could think of to contact."

Braddock did not seem at all surprised and replied,

"I know! To put your mind at rest, I received a phone call from your son Oliver telling me he was released by his friend Barry. Arrangements are being made to relocate your son to another part of Durham with round-the-clock police protection."

David could feel the tension drain from his body as he gave a huge sigh of relief.

"We are keeping your son's release under wraps for now so the abductors continue to think he is still tied up in the apartment. I have already informed DS Peterson of the developments. Peterson is at a crucial stage in locating Jackie, so Oliver's protection is vital if we are to rescue your daughter."

"Can I contact my son, Inspector?" asked David.

"Certainly, he still has his mobile phone, but I expect you will want to share the good news with Sarah without going into detail about the kidnapping."

"Of course! I will do that right away and thank you so much for what you and your colleagues are doing for us. Let us hope and pray that Peterson finds my daughter and ends this awful nightmare once and for all."

37

Peterson makes his move

Lady Greenwood and Jackie soon settled into their Villa overlooking Torquay Bay. Jackie was determined to make the most of the August sunshine and asked her Ladyship what the plans were for the day.

"What would you like to do?" asked her Ladyship.

"Now let me see," replied Jackie trying to look relaxed and happy. "What about a walk along the promenade, Mum? And whilst we are there, we could enjoy a vanilla ice cream."

"Sounds perfect," replied her Ladyship.

Jackie smiled and gave her Ladyship a hug, "I will slip into something nice and cool and rejoin you in the lounge, Mum."

Jackie's mind was in turmoil. Desperate to escape the clutches of Lady Greenway but, at the same time, knowing that any attempts to escape would put her brother in danger. If she ever got the opportunity to escape, thought Jackie, she was determined that the mysterious brown briefcase was going with her.

Peterson was excited when Google Maps pinpointed a Beach Crescent overlooking Torquay Bay. Hailing a taxi, he was soon on his way to the other side of the bay to find the location where, hopefully, Jackie was being held. His first intention was to hang around Beach Crescent and watch the comings and goings of the residents. Fifteen villas made up the crescent, so Peterson would have to find a spot where he could observe each residence.

Peterson had never seen Jackie in person, but the home videos he had seen back in Burnley and the photo would help him to distinguish between the many people entering and exiting each of the properties. An hour after his 9 o'clock arrival, his heart leapt as two ladies left a nearby villa; one was definitely Jackie. Fortunately, being near the promenade, they dismissed the driver standing by the limousine and made their way onto the seafront on foot. Jackie was smiling and linking arms with the other older lady, which puzzled Peterson for a moment, but he would not be deterred from trying to pass a note on to Jackie when the opportunity arose.

Keeping his distance, Peterson had no problem shadowing the two ladies as they made their way down the promenade. They sat down on the promenade benches occasionally, chatting and soaking up the sunshine. Peterson tried to sit on the same seat near Jackie a couple of times but was beaten to it by other members of the public. Biding his time, Peterson knew he had to be very careful and choose the right moment to pass on his note without drawing the attention of Jackie's companion, whom he assumed was Jackie's abductor. That moment came when they entered a café not far from Princess Pier. Following behind, Peterson heard Jackie asking her 'mum' if she would like an iced latte which again caused some consternation in the mind of Peterson. Mum? He thought. He was now wondering whether this was indeed Jackie and, looking again at the photograph, convinced himself to continue with his plan to pass on the note at the first opportunity.

Finding a table near Jackie, he ordered a coffee and hoped that she would use the lady's toilet. His hopes were realised when Jackie rose from her seat and went to the toilet after speaking to 'her mum'. As she passed Peterson's table, he knocked his coffee onto the floor, standing up immediately to apologise for nearly spoiling her summer dress.

"So sorry!" stuttered Peterson, and as they both bent down to pick up the pieces of broken crockery, Peterson attempted to slip the note into her hand. Initially, she withdrew her hand, thinking this clumsy idiot was being a bit over-familiar until she saw the note and quickly picked it up from where Peterson had dropped it on the floor.

Jackie sat on the toilet and anxiously read the crumpled note, 'Your brother Oliver is safe and well and under secure police protection.' Flushing the note down the toilet, she returned to her seat.

"What was all that about?" asked her Ladyship.

"Oh, just some clumsy idiot knocked his coffee over and nearly ruined my dress. No damage done."

Later that afternoon, her Ladyship and Jackie returned to their villa, leaving Peterson scratching his head about what to do next. Hanging on for a couple of hours on Beach Crescent and seeing no signs of Jackie making any move, he decided to return to his B&B for the night and resume his surveillance the next day.

38

Profitable encounter

Rising early, Peterson was soon making his way to Beach Crescent, thankful that the sun was shining again and confirming Torquay Bay's nickname of the English Riviera. Anticipating a long stay, he had brought a snack and a flask of coffee to keep the hunger pangs away. However, there would not be much time to enjoy his cheese roll or coffee as Jackie was coming down the steps of the villa and making her way to the promenade. Peterson could not believe the golden opportunity that now lay before him, but something told him to hold back and wait before trying to contact her. Allowing Jackie, who was wearing a bright yellow dress, to go a long way ahead, Peterson slowly began to follow, making sure he did not lose sight of her. She was now standing near the English Riviera Wheel; she hesitated to join the small waiting queue, looking around. When she saw Peterson approaching, she joined the holidaymakers, ensuring she was the last in the queue. Peterson realised her intentions and soon sat beside her as the wheel began rotating. Fortunately, they had a seat on the wheel to themselves.

"Hello, Jackie."

Jackie was extremely nervous, was this a trick and part of her Ladyship's network to test her, or was it really a knight in shining armour?

"My name is Peterson, and I am a policeman." His Geordie accent caused a look of suspicion from Jackie.

"What's a Geordie doing in Torquay?" she asked.

"I am a detective sergeant based at Burnley, and I have been given the task of trying to locate you for the past six months."

The relief on Jackie's face brought a beaming smile to Peterson's. There followed a few tears from Jackie, prompting Peterson to put a reassuring arm around this young girl who had endured months of fear and anguish.

"You called your abductor 'Mum', which caused me a bit of confusion."

"Oh, that? It's a role I have learned to play, and I think she's convinced I genuinely want to be her daughter; that is why I have been allowed out on my own today, plus the other small matter of the threat to kill my brother should I stray, but thanks to you and your police colleagues that's no longer an immediate threat."

He nodded. "We need to tread carefully now as we make plans for your escape if we are going to get you back to your mum and dad safely."

"You are not suggesting I try to escape now, are you, Mr Peterson? I don't think leaving Lady Greenway just now is a good idea. The network of drug smugglers and gangsters under her control needs to be brought to justice. My life and my family's life will always be in danger while this cartel continues to operate. I have plans to try and access important files and possibly obtain computer data that may help us to locate Lady Greenway's many contacts. I cannot be sure, but I am particularly interested in a briefcase that may contain the vital information you and your colleagues would be glad to get your hands on."

Peterson was in awe of her courage.

"I wouldn't want anything to happen to you now. Are you sure you want to go ahead with this?"

"I think so, Mr Peterson. You won't get another opportunity as good as this to smash this drugs' ring. If you were to organise a police raid on the villa now, my guess is that the evidence of all her contacts would be destroyed before you got there."

He looked across the Bay to admire the view, "I could really enjoy this ride on the wheel in different circumstances," and turning to Jackie, he suggested that they keep in touch daily and if for any reason she is not able to get out on any day to put some object on the windowsill of her room.

"There's a vase of yellow imitation flowers I could use; they should be easily seen."

As the ride on the Wheel came to a stop, Peterson and Jackie went their different ways, acting as though they were complete strangers.

39

Friendship restored

Back in Durham, Barry was so delighted to hear his friend's voice in answer to his telephone call.

"Thanks, Barry, for what you did the other day. I don't know how you found me in that strange flat, but I'm so glad you did. There's a copper outside my door, and I was just going to make him a cup of coffee when you rang. I can't reveal my location just now, only to say I am still in Durham and can pursue my studies online. I really miss you, Barry, and when this is all over, I promise to attend a Sunday morning service. I have already visited their website and heard a couple of sermons. You never know, Barry, your prayers may yet be answered."

"I am sure they will," replied Barry, hardly able to contain his joy at what he had just heard.

They chatted for another half hour before Oliver heard a call from outside the flat door,

"Where's my coffee?"

"Will have to go; please promise to ring again tomorrow, Barry, you are my only contact with the outside world."

40

Matrimony restored

Sarah greeted David with a warm embrace, seeming much more cheerful, having taken time to look her best and was especially appreciative of the flowers David handed to her. The trauma of Jackie's abduction had brought David and Sarah much closer together. Sitting on the sofa that same evening, David was trying to find the courage and the right moment to ask Sarah if they should end their separation and get back together permanently.

"Would you like some coffee, David?"

"Before you do that, please sit next to me; I need to ask you something before I lose my nerve."

Sarah complied as she held David's hand. He smiled,

"Er, I was wondering if we could end this separation and get back together permanently. I really miss you when we are not together and realise what a fool I've been ever to suggest the separation in the first place. Of course, if you want more time to think about it…"

She put her fingers to his lips and, much to David's surprise and joy, asked, "Are we moving into your place or mine?"

"Anywhere as long as I don't have to sleep on the sofa," he replied, which gave them both a good laugh.

David's phone rang,

"Hello David, this is Peterson. Just letting you know that things are moving fast down here in Torquay. I've spoken with Jackie today. You have an amazing daughter. She is okay, and we are working together to plan her escape. I can't go into details right now, but we are at a crucial stage, and I hope things can be wrapped up by the end of the week. I have spoken with Chief Inspector Braddock, and he has extended my stay here for one more week."

41

It's now or never

Jackie set her alarm for 5 am as she retired to bed. It was already past midnight, and her plan to search for the briefcase earlier had been thwarted by the late-night activity of a butler who never seemed to sleep.

The vibration of the mobile alarm stirred Jackie from her slumber. She quickly got out of bed and dressed, ready for the dangerous pursuit of the mysterious briefcase. She would have to forego her shower today; no time to waste. Creeping slowly along the corridor and up a flight of stairs to Lady Greenway's office, Jackie felt her heart beating fast. On entering the office, she sat down to calm herself and, after a brief rest, started her search for the briefcase. A good ten minutes later, there was still no briefcase to be found. Searching high and low for a concealed safe, her persistence was rewarded when seeing a picture on the wall slightly skewed, she lifted it from the wall and found the hidden safe. However, the safe was one thing, knowing the combination was another.

Jackie wondered whether to abandon her attempts to find the briefcase and make a run for it but realised that without exposing the people involved in the drug-running network, her life and that of her loved ones would always be in danger. Returning to her bedroom, she noticed the butler's bedroom door was slightly ajar.

Peering in, she could see he was fast asleep and snoring merrily, but more than that, the briefcase was lying by the side of the bed. She would never have another opportunity like this, so with her heart in her mouth, she entered the bedroom and slowly retrieved the briefcase. As she picked it up, it gave a slight jingling sound, the sound of rattling keys. The snoring abruptly stopped, and the butler began to move. After picking up the briefcase, Jackie did not hang around but fled down the stairs and made her way to the front entrance. The door, unfortunately, was locked. Desperately wondering what to do next, Jackie grabbed a chair, threw it against the bay window, and was soon running down the road.

Peterson drove to Beach Crescent and parked his car on the adjoining street. The weather wasn't at its best, but at least it was dry. As he turned the corner into the Crescent, he heard a shout; it was Jackie running at breakneck speed, holding onto a briefcase. The sound of gunfire followed. Peterson quickly grabbed Jackie's arm and almost yanked her off her feet, and both ran to his car. Looking in his driving mirror as they sped off, Peterson caught a glimpse of the butler, as he rounded the corner, stark naked, and firing his pistol at random, failing to hit them as his intended target.

Lady Greenway was absolutely furious when the butler dashed into her bedroom and informed her of Jackie's escape.

"Get out!" She screamed.

She staggered to the bathroom with her mind in a whirl, not knowing whether to lament the betrayal of her adopted daughter or the loss of vital information contained in the briefcase.

After dressing, she dashed to the dining room and gulped down her coffee.

"Get the car out and make sure Riley has the boat ready," she screamed.

The butler threw some clothes on and hastily left the building, glad to escape Lady Greenway's wrath. She tried desperately to remember the combination to the safe. Finally, after ten long minutes, the safe door opened, and she began stuffing wads of cash into a large suitcase.

On the way to the marina, the butler drove in silence but having told Lady Greenway that he managed to get the car registration number, her raging mood subsided slightly. Fortunately for her Ladyship, she still had all her contacts stored on her laptop, contacts throughout the UK who would do whatever she requested. She was soon emailing certain willing assassins, informing them that they must find the car and the occupants and retrieve the briefcase. She described them as male and female, and, if possible, the female to be kept alive and returned to a destination that would be made known later.

In order not to bring panic to all her contacts and complete disintegration of the whole drug network, Lady Greenway did not mention the ongoing fiasco to the majority of the members of the cartel.

A crew of six was on the schooner, including her

chaperone, who was still in Lady Greenway's bad books. There would be no halt to the drug network, with instructions continuing from the schooner directly to the independent drug lords under the supervision of Lady Greenway; there was too much money at stake to abandon this lucrative and, unfortunately for many, life-threatening trade.

As the schooner set sail, Lady Greenway's mood changed as the realisation of the loss of her adopted daughter began to sink in. She let out a loud wail and retired to her cabin in tears. After a couple of hours, her chaperone was getting rather impatient with her Ladyship's extended stays of absence and persisted in banging on her cabin door, reminding her that the drug barons needed her instructions and information if the network was to continue running smoothly. After she failed to respond, our loyal chaperone-come-butler was now so exasperated he bawled out at the top of his voice,

"Get a grip, your Ladyship! Or we shall lose a lot of money."

The cabin door swung open, and Lady Greenway's ashen, tear-drenched face appeared.

"You, my man, are becoming a liability, and if you continue banging on my door, will end up in the English Channel."

"Excuse me, your Ladyship but your infatuation with that girl will affect us all and put us all in danger. Why don't you accept that motherhood is not the greatest priority just now?"

On hearing that, she stared at her butler with eyes bulging and a face so red it looked like she was going to explode,

"Get out of my sight!" she screamed.

He knew he had now cooked his goose and would have to watch his back if he was going to survive the sea journey to their next destination.

The conflict between losing Jackie and trying to stay wealthy through involvement in the illicit drugs trade was taking its toll on Lady Greenway's mental health. She realised her chaperone was right in saying she needed to get a grip and, after much anguish and turmoil, resumed her duties masterminding the drug cartel.

That evening as the schooner made its way in the darkness through the choppy waters, Lady Greenway arrived on deck to try and control her seasickness. Her chaperone was also suffering leaning over the side of the boat bringing up his breakfast. Without a moment's hesitation and in a blinding rage, she gave him an almighty push and sent him flying overboard. The noise of the sea drowned out the screams as the poor man most certainly ended up in Davy Jones's Locker.

42

A great discovery

Finding a lay-by just outside Torquay, Peterson, with great urgency, rang Chief Inspector Braddock to tell him of their escape. Initially, Braddock was thrilled to hear that Jackie was out of the abductor's clutches but really worried about the predicament they were now in.

"I will inform the force in Somerset. In the meantime, I suggest you make your way to London, and I will try to arrange an appointment with the Home Secretary. We need to deal with this at the highest level if we are to bring this vast network of drug runners to justice. Keep off the motorway and try and take a country route to London and please, please take care."

Before setting off on their precarious journey, Peterson asked Jackie if she was happy with Chief Inspector Braddock's suggestion.

"Sure, this is really exciting. We might even see the Prime Minister!"

Peterson smiled. This young lady was going to be fun despite the danger they both faced.

"We must have a quick look in this briefcase before we go anywhere," he said.

Slipping on latex gloves, he opened the case and found some sheets of A4 paper, which didn't seem at all significant and a bunch of keys.

"Is that it?" wailed Jackie.

Peterson stuffed the contents back in the briefcase, wondering whether they had overestimated the significance and importance of this brown bag of innocuous items. She was about to throw the briefcase onto the back seat when she noticed something odd about the flap as she tried to close it.

"Hold on a minute, what's this inside the flap? Looks like a zip."

Releasing the zip and feeling inside the pocket, Jackie lifted her hand and, with a note of triumph, shrieked,

"Eureka! it's a hard drive backup disk."

Peterson did think about swallowing it for safekeeping but did not relish the thought of it coming out at the other end.

"We need to get a replacement for this disk to put back in the briefcase as soon as possible. Keep your eyes open for the next supermarket," he said and then drove off with the disk tucked down the side of his shoe.

It did not take long to find a supermarket just outside Newton Abbot. Having purchased an identical hard drive disc, they decided to have a snack in the café as Jackie was feeling rather peckish, having had no time for breakfast. With Jackie sufficiently nourished, they made their way to Exeter and then to Sidmouth, deciding that keeping as near to the coast as possible would be the best option.

After a while, Peterson started looking intently into his rear mirror.

"We are being followed."

The car behind began to pick up speed and was soon racing alongside theirs.

"Get your head down, Jackie!"

The bullet whistled through the open window, missing them both by inches. With a quick turn of the steering wheel, Peterson veered into the path of the pursuing car and managed to edge it off the road, where it finished up in a shallow ditch. Peterson and Jackie were not out of danger yet, but at least the pursuers would be out of action long enough to allow them to make a detour.

Turning off the A3052, they found themselves in a little hamlet called Harcombe. Peterson parked up in a layby and just sat there with a blank expression.

"Are you okay?" asked Jackie with some concern.

Wiping the sweat from his brow, he replied,

"I'm worried that I've made the wrong decision and should have contacted the local police authorities in Torquay. I've put your life in danger as well as mine."

Jackie smiled and held his hand.

"We will get through this, Matthew. I'm right behind you in your decision. We must get these thugs behind bars where they belong."

He seemed to perk up on hearing this.

"Seeing the cartel has our reg number, I suggest we abandon the car and make our way to London by other means?"

"I agree, even if we have to walk it," she replied, looking down at her flimsy footwear.

After a long walk, they came across a bus stop and waited a good half an hour before a bus arrived. They were not sure where it was going but decided to board it anyway as it was going in the right direction. A couple of bus changes later, they arrived in Axminster and, feeling weary from their trek, booked in for an overnight stay at the George Hotel.

43

Sniper

Oliver's phone rang, indicating Barry's call.

"Happy Birthday Oliver!"

"What! Is it September already? I had totally forgotten my birthday. Thanks, Barry."

Barry was just about to speak when he heard gunfire, followed by a long period of silence.

Oliver had dropped the phone and was cowering behind the bed when his apartment door opened and in staggered his guard, holding his arm now dripping with blood. He walked a few more paces and then collapsed on the floor, gun still in his hand.

"Oliver! What's going on?" Barry was frantically trying to know what the bangs were all about.

"My guard has been shot. I have already rung the emergency number, and the backup is on its way. I'll ring you back."

Wrapping one of his shirts around the guard's arm, Oliver picked up the gun and peered cautiously onto the landing. Whoever had done the shooting had left. He could hear the sirens wailing, and before long, the armed police warned Oliver that they were about to enter his room. The guard had been shot three times. Fortunately, two had hit his bulletproof vest, which undoubtedly saved his life.

Oliver was unceremoniously bundled into a waiting police car surrounded by three armed policemen and driven off to an unknown destination.

Back at the police headquarters in Durham, the Chief Inspector was scratching his head, trying to figure out how the gunman knew where Oliver was hiding.

44

London bound

Before settling down to enjoy an evening meal, Peterson rang Chief Inspector Braddock to fill him in on the latest developments.

"We had to abandon our car, Chief Inspector, as they are aware of the registration number, and after a skirmish on the A3052 with a hail of bullets, we managed to drive them off the road into a ditch. We abandoned the car in a place called Harcombe and are now staying overnight in the George Hotel, Axminster. We plan to make our way to London on public transport."

"Nay, lad! I suggest you hire a taxi and make sure you get a receipt. The policeman keeping watch over Jackie's brother was shot today, he will survive, but time is now of the essence, and the sooner you get to the Home Office with that hard drive disk, the sooner we will all be safer in our beds. I will leave it up to you whether you tell Jackie about the shooting incident. Oliver is okay and in another secret location."

Peterson felt unsure about getting a taxi as he now saw gangsters around every corner.

"I suggest we make our way to the bus depot and board a bus that takes us in the direction of London," he told Jackie.

She nodded in agreement, and to his surprise, she linked arms with him as they made their way to the bus terminal. Unfortunately, buses were in short supply; one was going to Lyme Regis, but that was no help.

In the meantime, Peterson's abandoned car had been discovered by two men, the same two men who had taken potshots at Peterson and Jackie. There were whoops of delight when they found the briefcase still containing the hard drive disc. However, not content with their valuable, unknown to them, useless find, they decided to continue their pursuit and fulfil Lady Greenway's wishes to destroy the two vital dangerous witnesses for good. Armed with guns and carrying photographs of their intended targets, they headed for Axminster.

Peterson and Jackie made their way to the taxi rank as they could think of no alternative means of getting to London.

"Sorry mate, no taxis available for at least an hour or so; I suggest you come back then. There's a nice café around the corner."

Peterson nodded, and they both decided a snack would be a good idea before embarking on their journey to London.

The café wasn't too busy, and having found a table, they tried to relax and enjoy a welcome cup of coffee, lasagne, and a side salad.

"May I borrow your phone, Matthew? I'm desperate to let my mum and dad know I am okay; a text will do for now."

He handed her his phone and tucked into his meal. The café window was directly in front of him, and as he munched happily on his lasagne, he nearly choked as a distinctive midnight blue Mercedes drove past the window. There was no doubt in his mind that their pursuers were back on their trail. Jackie was unaware of the danger they were now in as she concentrated on the mobile phone and her text message.

Peterson's problem now was how to get to the taxi rank without being seen by their assassins. Jackie handed the mobile back to him, unaware of the drama unfolding.

"We need to find the back entrance to this place, Jackie, just as a precaution."

She thought he was being a bit too cautious and was about to head for the front door when Peterson grabbed her arm and led her to the toilets.

"Sorry, Jackie, but we must find another way out of here. Trust me."

The proprietor wasn't too happy about Peterson's request, but when he showed her his police identity card, she complied and led them through the kitchen and into the backyard.

45

Desperate measures

"Hi, Oliver! Where have they taken you now?"

Barry had been told of the attempt on Oliver's life and that of his police protection officer and was anxious to know if his friend was okay and where he was now situated.

"I can't divulge that information, Barry. I can say that I am somewhere in Yorkshire. But I won't be here much longer as I plan to abscond at the first opportunity."

Barry was aghast at Oliver's intention to abandon his police protection.

"Don't do that, Oliver! You will endanger your life. From what I have heard, they are very near to locating Jackie."

"Some protection! I think I need protection from the police or some informer within the police setup. I understand your concern, but I must try and make myself incognito and go where no one knows where I am. I have a few ideas. I suggest your pray to your God for me."

"Oliver, why don't you pray yourself? I don't have a monopoly on God's grace. He will hear you if you call on Him."

"I might just do that, Barry. If the police can't protect me, he is probably the only one who can."

The phone call ended abruptly, leaving Barry extremely worried for Oliver's safety. Barry would now need to draw on his fledgling faith and take all his worries and anxieties to the God he had come to know and believe in.

46

Kind farmers

Peterson and Jackie cautiously approached the back entrance of the taxi office. Seeing the coast was clear, they settled in the waiting room, awaiting their turn for a taxi due in five minutes. Jackie was desperate for the toilet and decided it would be wise to use one now before their long journey to London.

But when she returned to the waiting room, she was slightly bewildered to find that Peterson was no longer there. Perhaps he had gone to the toilet, she thought and sat down to wait.

"Your taxi is ready," called out the receptionist.

"Thank you!" replied Jackie. "Be with you in a minute."

She stood by the toilet door and called out Peterson's name; there was no answer. Returning to her seat, Jackie noticed a familiar object on the floor under the seat: the hard drive disc. Something is not right here, she thought and asked the receptionist if she had seen anything of Peterson.

"There were three men in the reception room, but I didn't see them leave as I was on the telephone."

Edging her way past the taxis and keeping well concealed, Jackie saw the damaged Mercedes with the engine ticking over and Peterson being bundled into the back seat. She felt her heart skip a beat and made the hard decision to leave the premises via the back entrance. The priority, and she was sure that Peterson would agree, was to ensure the drug cartel did not get their hands on the hard drive disc. Jackie eventually left Axminster behind, making her way through woodland in the direction of Yeovil.

In the meantime, one of the pursuers, gun cocked in his pocket, returned to the taxi rank to capture Jackie, but she had already made her escape. The pursuers spent the next half an hour driving around the back streets of Axminster, and realising that she had given them the slip, they turned their attention back to Peterson. They bound him up and secured him in the back seat, saying they would deal with him later, then drove off at breakneck speed, onto the A358.

Jackie arrived on the outskirts of Yeovil at about 7 pm. The twenty miles or so across fields and woodland had taken its toll, especially on her feet, which were now beginning to blister. Deciding that entering the centre of Yeovil would be too risky, she turned aside and entered a farmyard, hoping to find somewhere to rest.

"Can I help you?" The voice from behind gave Jackie a start and she spun round to see a man carrying a spade and whose clothes were caked in cow muck.

The young man gave her a smile. "Sorry for the unpleasant smell, but it's one of the hazards of being a dairy farmer, I'm afraid."

"I should apologise for venturing onto your land uninvited," replied Jackie. "I am afraid I have lost my way and would appreciate your help in showing me how to find my way back to the nearest bus stop."

"Certainly, but you look like you are in need of a sit-down and a nice hot drink. I would be so pleased if you would join my wife and me for supper."

Jackie did not need to be asked twice and followed the farmer to his cottage, where she was met with the inviting smell of baked bread and a very convivial lady and two children.

After the farmer had explained to his wife that Jackie needed some refreshments, she was led to a large kitchen and told to make herself at home. The warm welcome, log fire, and the aroma of the freshly baked bread lifted her spirits, and sitting down, she soon enjoyed homemade soup, the delicious bread, and a refreshing cup of ground coffee.

When she was suitably refreshed, they all sat in front of the log fire with the two daughters, aged about eleven and fifteen, sitting on either side of Jackie.

"My name is Tom, and this is Elsie, and these two helpers are Janet and Joan."

Jackie smiled and thanked them for their warm hospitality, stifling a yawn.

"Where do you come from?" asked the eldest child.

"A long way from here," replied Jackie.

"You have a funny accent; my guess is you come from Yorkshire."

"Now, children, that's enough for today," intervened the farmer's wife, much to Jackie's relief.

"Come along, Tom and you children too. This young lady needs to rest."

Elsie then brought out a blanket and covered Jackie, who was soon fast asleep.

There was lots of whispering in the children's bedroom later.

"I think she is running away from someone," whispered Joan, the youngest of the two. "Maybe it's the law, or she could be a spy. We might be in danger; I think we need to inform the police."

"Oh, go to sleep; I think your imagination is running away with you," replied Janet.

But Janet could not sleep, and Joan's silly talk had set her mind racing. What if she really is on the run? By 2 am, Janet had allowed her fear to overcome her reason and decided to let a friend know of their worry about the stranger in their house; she clicked 'send' on her mobile and promptly went to sleep.

Jackie awoke from her slumber the following morning and for a moment or two wondered where she was. She was, however, thankful for undisturbed sleep and ready for a nice mug of the coffee she could smell coming from the stove. The farmer's wife had already put the eggs in the frying pan and informed Jackie that breakfast would soon be ready. Tom had been up for an hour or so tending to the cows. After folding the blanket and placing it on the back of the chair, Jackie glanced through the window and saw a police car pull up outside the farm. This was not what Jackie wanted to see, and before the two policemen arrived at the door, she withdrew behind the curtains. The farmer's wife was curious to know why the police had called and wondered whether some of the farming equipment had been stolen.

"Good morning, madam," greeted the policeman, looking a little anxious.

"Can I help you?" responded Elsie.

"We have been informed that you have a visitor, and we were wondering if everything is okay?" the sergeant replied.

"Why shouldn't it be?" questioned Elsie, looking surprised.

From the corner of her eye, Elsie could see Jackie putting her finger to her lips.

"The visitor you refer to left last night. I think she was on her way to Torquay. Is the young lady in trouble?"

"No, madam, do you mind if we come in and make sure all is well?"

"I do mind, and unless you have a warrant, I would like you to leave now."

As the police drove away, Jackie approached Elsie and, holding her hand, thanked her, saying that when Tom had finished tending to the cows, she would explain the reason why she had stumbled onto their farm.

Tom returned to the farm mid-afternoon. When he was settled, Elsie called Jackie into the sitting room.

"Jackie has something to tell us."

Jackie then began to explain the whole saga, from the time she was kidnapped to her visit to their farm. Tom and Elsie listened in amazement, and when Jackie had finished, Elsie put her arm around her and hugged her.

"I am really worried about Sergeant Peterson, but there is not much I can do for him now."

Tom asked what the number of the crook's car was again and, after making a note of it, began dialling various numbers on his phone.

Two hours later, Tom's phone rang,

"We have spotted the car on the outskirts of the town near Robertson's farm; all available tractors are on their way."

Tom leapt to his feet, asking Jackie to follow. With both securely on board the tractor, they made their way to Robertson's farm. By the time they arrived, seven tractors were already there blocking the assailants' car. One of the crooks waved his gun in the air, but after one of the tractors ran over the bonnet of the car, reducing the front of it to a heap of mangled metal, he put the pistol on the ground. Jackie was soon running to see if Peterson was okay and, much to her delight, saw him, with his hands bound, clambering out of the back of the car only to be smothered with Jackie's outstretched arms and drenched in her tears of joy.

Deciding what to do with the two assailants was a bit of a problem, but in the end, Peterson suggested that they let them go. Calling the police to apprehend them would cause more problems than it was worth; they would not be going far without transport and to make sure they emptied their pockets of all their belongings.

Tom wanted Peterson and Jackie to return to his farm for a meal before they resumed their journey, but Peterson said that time was of the essence as they needed to get to London as soon as possible. Thanking Tom and the rest of the farmers, they promised to get back in touch when everything was sorted, and their lives were back to normal. One of the farmers suggested he gave them a lift to Salisbury, bawling it out rather unwisely and loud enough to be heard by the two rogues. Still, it was a welcome lift taking them almost to the centre of the town and finding the Kings Head Hotel, they decided to stay there for the night.

47

A turning point in the life of Oliver

Oliver, finding himself on the outskirts of York with very little money, decided to try and get back to his mum and dad. After a long walk, he arrived in York only to find that the train fare and the alternative bus fare to Manchester were too much. With only fifteen pounds in his wallet, his only option was to return to Durham and ask Barry if he would let him stay for a few days. The fare was fourteen pounds, leaving Oliver with one pound in his pocket.

He sat at the rear of the bus, making himself inconspicuous and keeping his head down most of the way. The hood on his jacket helped to keep his face hidden, and arriving at Barry's in one piece, he knocked on his door. Barry nearly fell over on seeing his friend Oliver.

"Well, I don't believe it. What are you doing here?" Barry guided Oliver to the sofa and sat him down.

Barry then realised the implications of his friend's visit and went to the window to glance into the street.

"It's okay, Barry; I wasn't followed. I am in desperate need of help," and holding up the pound coin, explained that it was all he had.

"I am glad you came, Oliver. I have been worried sick about you, and of course, I will help you; after all, what are friends for?"

Oliver thanked Barry for his help and friendship and, at the same time, apologised for the danger he had now put his friend in.

Oliver slept soundly that night. The October sunshine coming through the curtains shone on his face giving him a feeling of a new dawn. Things can only get better from now on, he thought. The bedroom door was slightly ajar, with a view into the sitting room revealing Barry in a kneeling position which alarmed Oliver.

"Are you okay, Barry!"

Barry responded by turning round and giving Oliver a smile.

"Fine, thanks, Oliver. A very good morning to you. Coffee and toast coming up."

As Barry closed the book on the dining table, Oliver realised that Barry had been praying and reading his Bible.

After dressing and drawing up to the table, Oliver asked Barry what he had been reading from the Bible today.

"The Epistle to the Philippians chapter 4. Verses 6 and 7 are particularly relevant, considering our present circumstances."

"So, are you going to tell me what they say?"

"They tell us not to be anxious. The exact words are:

Be anxious for nothing, but in everything by prayer and supplication, with thanksgiving, let your requests be made known to God; and the peace of God, which surpasses all understanding, will guard your hearts and minds through Christ Jesus.

"I understand the apostle Paul had Roman garrisons in mind when he wrote these words. So just like a Roman garrison would guard a position from the enemy, God will set a guard around his saints and grant them divine protection. All we have to do is ask God for it and thank him, resulting in freedom from fear and a settled peace."

"That is easier said than done, isn't it?" asked Oliver.

"I admit it is something that you have to learn, and I am a learner, but either God is who says he is, or he is no God at all. God has promised to give us the faith to believe his promises, which I am increasingly realising each day. We who are of little faith can have a faith that can move mountains, according to the teachings of Jesus."

"They threw Christians to the lions in Roman times. Where was God then?"

Barry thought for a moment. "Good question. I don't know all the answers, Oliver, but I do remember a Bible study I attended, and the speaker was saying that the blood of the martyrs was the seed of the church. In other words, the sacrifice of the early martyrs helped to extend the church far and wide. Sometimes God allows his children to suffer for reasons known only to him.

You can guarantee, however, that God does not make mistakes. This is where faith again has to be put into action."

"Am I under his protection, seeing I am not a Christian yet?"

"You can be; that's up to you. Jesus wept over Jerusalem, saying he would have gathered them as a hen gathers her chicks, but they were not willing. Jerusalem was destroyed in AD 70 by the Romans. The challenge here is whether you are willing to submit your life and future to Jesus Christ."

"If you keep talking like that, Barry, you will convince me that I, too, need to become a Christian."

"Oliver, that request was on my prayer list this morning," answered Barry, smiling.

Barry decided to change the subject as he did not want to antagonise his friend at this stage.

"I think you need to let your mum and dad know you are okay. The police might contact them in trying to find you," said Barry.

"That's a good idea; I will phone them now."

"Hello, Mum, Oliver here. Just to let you know, I am safe and sound. I am letting you know that since the shooting of the one who was supposed to be protecting me, I have withdrawn myself from the safe house. I would appreciate it if you would ring the police protection team and let them know I am okay. I don't want to use my phone as I don't want them to trace the call back to me. Love you, Mum, and tell Dad I love him too."

Oliver's mum was overjoyed to hear that her son was safe but worried that he was even in more danger.

"Please take care, Oliver," pleaded Sarah.

"I am in God's hands now, Mum, so don't worry."

Barry could not help but smile when he heard the last remark. But Barry's smile turned into a gasp of horror as the apartment window shattered as a bullet flew across the room, knocking Oliver to the floor and leaving him writhing in agony. Blood was everywhere. Sarah's voice screamed from the phone,

"What's happened? Oliver! What's happened?"

Barry had already dashed into the kitchen to grab a couple of tea towels and was soon stemming the blood which had been flowing from Oliver's right shoulder. Picking Oliver's phone off the floor, Barry desperately tried to dial 999 and, after fumbling with his free hand, successfully got through to the switchboard.

"Emergency, someone has been shot. We need an ambulance quickly."

Oliver was pale but conscious.

"Someone must have been using telescopic sights on their firearm," muttered Oliver with a faint smile. "Don't worry, Barry, I don't blame God."

"You might not do, but I have serious doubts now."

"Don't, Barry; there must be a reason, which God will probably reveal later."

Barry shook his head, not in despair, but at Oliver's response to the whole situation. Oliver seemed to have more faith than himself just now. Barry was aghast at what had just happened to his friend.

"Hold on, Oliver; the ambulance is on its way."

The ambulance arrived within ten minutes, accompanied by armed police in cars everywhere. After the medics had examined Oliver, their initial conclusion was that the bullet had missed the vital organs and that Barry's tea towels probably saved Oliver's life.

"He'll live," were the parting assuring words from the medic as Oliver was wheeled out to the ambulance.

In the meantime, Barry redialled Sarah to tell her that Oliver had been shot, but the medics did not think it was serious. He would keep her informed when he had further news.

That evening Barry called in at the University Hospital in Durham to see how Oliver was coping.

"Hi, Barry; good to see you."

Oliver was sitting up in bed with tubes attached all over the place.

"I go into theatre tomorrow to get stitched up. The bullet went through my shoulder, missed my lungs, and broke no bones. You might find the bullet embedded in the wall. If the police don't want it as evidence, keep it for me as a souvenir. Your God is a good shot. Seriously, Barry, I could have been killed today, and where would I have gone then, I ask? Heaven or hell?"

"Well, I don't know the answer to that, Oliver; it will be one or the other. But this I do know if you really believe Jesus Christ to be your Saviour, you will be going to the same place as I am going, heaven."

"I believe, Barry."

Barry could not contain himself and, flinging his arms around Oliver, got entangled in tubes and wires at the same time. They both laughed together, the laughter of sheer joy.

The police guard popped his head around the door and bawled,

"Is everything all right?"

48

A very eventful train ride

Peterson felt much better after his welcome night's sleep, and on reaching the dining room, he found Jackie already munching on her cornflakes.

"Good morning, Jackie," Peterson stifled a yawn and sat down.

"Good morning, Matt. Hope you slept well?"

"Like a baby," he replied.

After finishing a hearty breakfast, Peterson was on the phone to Braddock, keeping him updated on all the recent developments. After finishing the conversation, he turned to Jackie.

"We must get moving as soon as we have checked out of here. I suggest we take a risk, catch the train to London, and get this vital information to the Home Office."

He did not mention the information given by Braddock of the attempt on Oliver's life but would tell her at a more opportune moment. Poor girl had enough to worry about just now.

The train was not due to leave for an hour and would take approximately an hour and a half to reach Waterloo Station.

Meanwhile, the two assailants, though unable to fulfil their mission of getting rid of Peterson and Jackie, were happy to still have the hard drive disc and intended to send the good news to Lady Greenway. After a long walk into town, they entered the local library to use one of their computers.

"I don't believe this!"

The colour drained from the faces of the two crooks as they realised they had been duped, ending up with an empty disc.

"Come on!" bawled one of them and racing out of the library, they grabbed the car keys from an elderly gentleman as he was about to enter his car, knocking him to the ground. They raced off, ignoring red traffic lights and any pedestrians that got in their way and were soon on their way to Salisbury.

The train was not too crowded, and Peterson and Jackie were able to find a corner seat to themselves. Peterson was relieved when the train started to move off. Jackie snuggled up to him, which seemed so natural and pleased the young Detective Sergeant as he reached out his hand to hold onto hers.

"Don't look now, but I think we have company," he said.

He had just seen two familiar faces enter from the opposite compartment, and they had already seen him. Sitting in the seat behind, they let it be known that unless Peterson handed over the disc, he would be leaving the train head first with a bullet in his brain.

"If that happens, the disc will be leaving with me as I just happen to have swallowed it," replied Peterson.

"Oh, you have you? In that case, we shall get off at the next station. We can always disembowel you," smirked one of the assailants.

"I have a better idea," the brighter of the two suggested. "Shove a load of laxatives down him; we are in no hurry."

With a gun poking in Peterson's back, they had no alternative but to comply with the crooks' wishes and leave the train at Basingstoke station. One of the assailants was already on his phone, and within 15 minutes, a police officer arrived and was soon directing them to a waiting car outside the railway station.

"Excuse me, but can I see your warrant card?" asked Peterson.

The police officer gave Peterson a push and ordered him to get in the car, yanking Jackie in at the same time. As they drove off, Peterson turned to his unpleasant assailants and smiled,

"You are not very good at being crooks, are you? I left the disc down the back of one of the train seats. So, what are the chances the cleaner will find it and hand it to the police authorities? Maybe it will stay there forever, maybe not."

The squint-eyed assailant turning to his partner asked if his idiot friend had any more bright ideas.

"Are you sure you haven't swallowed it?" asked the

not-so-bright one.

Peterson smiled, "I will enjoy watching you dissect my poo later."

"This is ridiculous," wailed the corrupt police officer. "We need to make our way to Waterloo station sharpish." And with a mighty swerve and U-turn, headed for London.

The train had already reached Waterloo by the time they arrived. One of the assailants shoved his colleague out of the car.

"Go and get the flipping disc before we all end up in Pentonville, and don't forget to get a platform ticket!"

Not very wisely, the not-so-bright one jumped over the ticket barrier and bounded towards the stationary train. He got on the train okay but had difficulty getting off as two British Transport police were waiting to apprehend him. However, he managed to give them the slip and raced toward his waiting friends. The Transport police were much more nimble, and before he could climb in the car, they had already grabbed him by the scruff of the neck.

During the commotion, Peterson grabbed Jackie's hand, and both ran from the car and were soon mingling among the crowds on their way down Belvedere Road.

"What about the disc?" asked Jackie frantically.

"Why do you think I am limping?" replied Peterson, smiling. "Don't worry, it's still in my shoe."

49

The Home Office

After a long walk down to Westminster Bridge and onto Parliament Street, they eventually reached Downing Street. Brushing past the police officer, Peterson wasted no time banging on the door of Number Ten.

As the door opened, Peterson held up his warrant card and demanded to see the Home Secretary.

"Sorry, my man, but you have come to the wrong address; the Minister of State does not reside here. You need Marshall Street."

"Where's that?" Peterson bawled.

"The other side of China Town, off Regent Street," replied the doorman.

"Come on, Jackie; we need to hurry!"

The police officer who had been observing the situation and was on the point of arresting Peterson, asked him what the problem was.

"You need to speak to my superior in Burnley; maybe that will help you understand what's going on."

The phone conversation with Chief Superintendent Braddock convinced the police officer that Peterson needed his help and was soon on the phone ordering a police patrol car.

When they arrived at the Home Office, an official greeted them and ushered them into the building. They were both led to a large office and greeted by the Minister of State for Crime, who, after ordering them coffee, made a remarkable statement:

"We were worried about you two. We are so glad you have made it, and now I believe you have something for me?"

Peterson hesitated momentarily and then asked the Minister what he knew about the reason for their visit.

"There is a massive organised national drug cartel operating throughout the country, and it is only recently that we have been able to follow any leads. We have apprehended some drug dealers, mainly Albanians, but the main organisers have eluded us so far."

"How do I know you are not part of the cartel?" asked Peterson with slight apprehension.

"I appreciate your caution, Peterson, but I can assure you the information you pass on to me will be dealt with at the highest level. To put your mind at rest, I intend to contact the Prime Minister through our video link, and he will confirm the authenticity of my credentials."

And true to his word, the Prime Minister appeared on the screen. Peterson and Jackie were a bit overawed at speaking directly to the Prime Minister but glad and relieved that, at last, they had completed their remarkable journey.

Taking his shoe and sock off, Peterson handed the hard drive disc to the Minister, who could not wait to connect the disc to the laptop and even allowed Peterson and Jackie the privilege of seeing the long list of contacts roll down the screen. Hundreds of names, email addresses, and telephone numbers. One particular name that interested Jackie more than all of them put together was Lady Greenway. However, when her name came up, there were no contact details.

50

Six months later

Peterson saw a lot of Jackie in the following months, and as their relationship progressed from deep friendship to a greater romantic attachment, this put Peterson in a quandary. Peterson was a practising Christian, but due to the pressure of work, was less committed to his faith and church attendance than he should have been. To marry an unbeliever was against the teachings of his Christian faith, so Peterson, much to his utter disappointment, decided to see less of Jackie. Jackie, however, had fallen head over heels in love with him and was at a loss as to why he was making vain excuses each time she suggested a meet-up. After much anguish and heart-searching, Peterson explained his dilemma to Jackie.

The final get-together would be an evening meal in the local restaurant. Jackie looked absolutely stunning when she turned up at the restaurant, causing Peterson's heart to ache with a deep longing to hold her and not let go. As they were led to their table and sat down, they were both feeling tense, and it was Jackie who spoke first,

"Matthew, can you tell me what's going on?"

"I am sorry, Jackie, but I have a problem I should have shared with you months ago. I am a practising

Christian and, therefore, cannot continue our relationship other than being good friends."

"But Matthew, I am a Christian and a member of the local Baptist Church."

Peterson's heart leapt, "Do you mean to tell me I have been having sleepless nights for nothing?"

"Yes, Matthew, for absolutely nothing. The only problem is that you had better be a good Baptist."

"I am Presbyterian, actually, but if you allow me that concession, would you consider spending your future with me?"

"Is that a proposal?"

"Yes, and if the answer is yes, I will probably faint on the spot."

The waiter waited patiently for the embrace to end and finally and with a smile, asked if they were ready to place their order.

Meanwhile, I expect you may be wondering whether Barry's prayers were answered regarding Oliver and his desire to see his good friend fully commit himself to the Lordship of Jesus Christ. The answer to that question is that they certainly were. Oliver and Barry were both baptised in the Baptist church in Durham and though initially, there was some antagonism from friends, the change in David and Barry could not be denied.

Hopes were high in the heart of David that many of the student community would one day see the relevance of the Christian faith in a very uncertain and insecure world. And, by the way, the lad whose bike was taken from him by Barry in pursuit of the kidnappers accepted Barry's apology and was happy to have his bike back in one piece. In completing their degrees, David and Barry became heavily involved in a drug support organisation associated with their local church in Durham, but that is another story.

51

Lady Greenway

The information on the disc led to hundreds of arrests, from the insignificant to the most prominent members of society. The drugs seized from various parts of the country had a total street value of five billion pounds. Some of the drug cartel members were members of the police and even important government civil servants. Some managed to flee the country, but extradition measures were already in place, and they would not escape justice for much longer.

The wedding of the year, as far as Peterson and Jackie were concerned, was held the following year at St Stephen's in the early Spring. Peterson sat nervously in the pew accompanied by his best man, Oliver. Some police colleagues and a very happy Barry were on hand to share in the ushering.

Jackie looked stunning as she entered the church accompanied by her dad, and a very proud mum was already wiping a tear from her eye, sitting proudly in the front pew.

The reception went well, especially Oliver's excellent speech. Oliver proved much more humorous than even Barry expected, but also, there were serious moments of reflection as he related the journey beginning on that fateful winter's night on the Pennine moor to the present happy day.

The next day following the enjoyable reception, the Ferry left Holyhead, Anglesey, for Belfast, where Peterson and Jackie would spend their honeymoon. The Leonardo Hotel proved to be an excellent location, and both Peterson and Jackie could not have been happier.

The following morning while enjoying a delightful breakfast, Jackie suddenly stopped eating and, staring wide-eyed across the room, put her hand on Peterson's and motioned her gaze to a table in the corner; two police officers were slipping handcuffs on a solitary lady sitting in the corner of the room; it was Lady Greenway. Lady Greenway had not noticed either Jackie or Peterson and when Jackie approached her table, she almost fainted on the spot. Jackie motioned to the police officers and asked if she could speak to Lady Greenway before they took her away and after Peterson displayed his warrant card, they agreed.

"Hello, Mum!"

Lady Greenway could not reply for a few minutes and stared at Jackie open-mouthed.

"My dear Jackie, how lovely to see you especially looking so happy and well."

Jackie took hold of Peterson's hand.

"I want you to meet my husband, Detective Sergeant Matthew Peterson."

"Pleased to meet you, Lady Greenway," he said, "pity it is not in better circumstances."

The net had closed on the main organiser of one of the largest drug cartels the United Kingdom had ever known. There was a tinge of sadness in the heart of Jackie, but then she remembered that this lady had no qualms about having her and Peterson eliminated to save her own skin.

Back in England, Peterson was proud of his police commendation and even more pleased to be married to the bravest and prettiest girl in the world.

The trial of Lady Greenway was held a few months later. She was sentenced to life imprisonment with no chance of parole. Not that she would serve her full sentence as she had been diagnosed with ovarian cancer and, within a few months of her jail sentence, lay dying in hospital under an armed guard. Lying there on her deathbed, she had a rare visitor. It was Jackie.

"Hello, Mum."

Lady Greenway's expression broke out into a look of surprise and, at the same time, one of joy, remarkable in the light of her serious illness and as Jackie held her hand, Lady Greenway whispered faintly,

"I am so sorry, Jackie."

Jackie remained with Lady Greenway for the next hour or so. Lady Greenway was finding it difficult to speak, but when she did manage, Jackie heard her repeat the word 'sorry' several times. Jackie held onto her hand and stroked her hair, trying hard to comfort her in her dying moments.

"Dear Lady Greenway, I forgive you for what you did to my family and me, but the one you should really be saying sorry to is the only one who can truly forgive you."

In between fighting for her next breath, Lady Greenway looked puzzled and replied, "And who might that be, Jackie?"

"The one who was crucified in order to save sinners like you and me."

"It's too late for that, Jackie," and in a low whisper, she managed to finish her sentence, "I have ruined too many lives, and anyway, there is no time now to make amends for my past mistakes."

"Many, worse than you, have asked God for forgiveness in their dying hours and died in peace. No one is beyond redemption if they are truly repentant."

"It sounds too good to be true, Jackie." And after another struggle to speak continued, "However, I am sorry and wish I could turn the clock back, but what I have done, I have done and must suffer the consequences."

"No! No! Lady Greenway. The door is still open to God's mercy."

But before Jackie could continue to share Lady Greenway's only eternal hope of redemption, Lady Greenway's laboured breathing fell silent, leaving Jackie distraught. Kissing Lady Greenway on the lifeless forehead, Jackie left the hospital and, on meeting

Matthew outside the hospital entrance, fell into his arms and began to sob uncontrollably, soaking his jacket with many tears.

Appendix

For readers in the UK who have a drug addiction problem, the following advice is featured on an NHS website.

Where to get help for drugs

A GP is a good place to start. They can discuss your problems with you and get you into treatment.

They may offer you treatment at the practice or refer you to your local drug service.

If you're uncomfortable talking to a GP, you can approach your local drug treatment service.

Visit the Frank website to find support near you.

If you're having trouble finding the right help, call the Frank drugs helpline on 0300 123 6600. They can talk you through all your options.

Charity and private drugs treatment

As well as the NHS, there are charities and private drug and alcohol treatment organisations that can help you.

Visit the Adfam website page, Finding Support, to see a list of useful organisations.

Private drug treatment can be expensive, but sometimes people get referrals through their local NHS.

Your first appointment

At your first appointment for drug treatment, the staff will ask you about your drug use. They'll also ask about your work, family and housing situation.

You may be asked to provide a sample of urine or saliva.

Staff will talk you through your treatment options and agree on a treatment plan with you.

They can tell you about local support groups for drug users and their families or carers.

You'll also be given a key worker who will support you throughout your treatment.

What drug treatment involves

Your treatment will depend on your personal circumstances and what you're addicted to. Your keyworker will work with you to plan the right treatment for you.

Your treatment plan may include a number of different treatments and strategies.

Talking therapies

Talking therapies, such as CBT, help you to see how your thoughts and feelings affect your behaviour.

Treatment with medicines

If you depend on heroin or another opioid, you may be offered a substitute drug, such as methadone or buprenorphine.

This means you can get on with your treatment without worrying about withdrawing or buying street drugs.

Detoxification (detox)

This is for people who want to stop taking opioids like heroin completely. It helps you to cope with the withdrawal symptoms.

Self-help

Some people find support groups like UKNA (Narcotics Anonymous) helpful. Your keyworker can tell you where your nearest group is.

Reducing harm

Your local drug service staff will help reduce the risks associated with your drug-taking. For example, you may be offered testing and treatment for hepatitis or HIV and AIDS.

Where you'll have your treatment

You may have your treatment while living at home or as a hospital inpatient.

If your drug-related problems are severe or complicated, you may be referred to a residential rehabilitation service.

These suggestions are very helpful in dealing with the problem of drug addiction. However, to really deal with addictions, whether it be alcohol, gambling, pornography, or drug abuse, is the need for a change of lifestyle or, to be more precise a changed life that can only happen through faith in Jesus Christ. In my younger days, my addictions were alcohol and gambling. My encounter with a work colleague who had been converted through a Billy Graham crusade in Manchester, England, completely changed my life. His enthusiasm and witness to his faith in Christ were intoxicating, and over two years, he convinced me that I, too, could change with the help of God's grace. My conversion happened sixty years ago, and my faith is still as vibrant as ever. Trials and challenges have been part of my earthly pilgrimage, including my wife being afflicted with multiple sclerosis, but even in our darkest moments, God has remained faithful.

Available worldwide from Amazon

Michael Terence Publishing

www.mtp.agency

mtp.agency

@mtp_agency

Printed in Great Britain
by Amazon

25823706R00108